One That Came Back

Hades' Spawn Motorcycle Club, Volume 3

Lexy Timms

Published by Dark Shadow Publishing, 2015.

Also by Lexy Timms

Alpha Bad Boy Motorcycle Club Triology
Alpha Biker

Conquering Warrior Series
Ruthless

Diamond in the Rough Anthology
Billionaire Rock
Billionaire Rock - part 2

Dominating PA Series
Her Personal Assistant - Part 1
Her Personal Assistant - Part 2
Her Personal Assistant - Part 3
Her Personal Assistant Box Set

Firehouse Romance Series
Caught in Flames
Burning With Desire
Craving the Heat
Firehouse Romance Complete Collection

Fortune Riders MC Series
Billionaire Biker
Billionaire Ransom
Billionaire Misery

Hades' Spawn Motorcycle Club
One You Can't Forget
One That Got Away

One That Came Back
One You Never Leave
Hades' Spawn MC Complete Series

Heart of the Battle Series
Celtic Viking
Celtic Rune
Celtic Mann
Heart of the Battle Series Box Set

Justice Series
Seeking Justice
Finding Justice
Chasing Justice
Pursuing Justice
Justice - Complete Series

Love You Series
Love Life: Billionaire Dance School Hot Romance
Need Love
My Love

Managing the Bosses Series
The Boss
The Boss Too
Who's the Boss Now
Love the Boss
I Do the Boss
Wife to the Boss
Employed by the Boss
Brother to the Boss
Senior Advisor to the Boss
Forever the Boss
Gift for the Boss - Novella 3.5

Christmas With the Boss

Moment in Time

Highlander's Bride

Victorian Bride

Modern Day Bride

A Royal Bride

Forever the Bride

R&S Rich and Single Series

Alex Reid

Parker

Saving Forever

Saving Forever - Part 1

Saving Forever - Part 2

Saving Forever - Part 3

Saving Forever - Part 4

Saving Forever - Part 5

Saving Forever - Part 6

Saving Forever Part 7

Saving Forever - Part 8

Southern Romance Series

Little Love Affair

Siege of the Heart

Freedom Forever

Soldier's Fortune

Tattooist Series

Confession of a Tattooist

Surrender of a Tattooist

Heart of a Tattooist

Tennessee Romance

Whisky Lullaby
Whisky Melody
Whisky Harmony

The Debt
The Debt: Part 1 - Damn Horse
The Debt: Complete Collection

The University of Gatica Series
The Recruiting Trip
Faster
Higher
Stronger
Dominate
No Rush

T.N.T. Series
Troubled Nate Thomas - Part 1
Troubled Nate Thomas - Part 2
Troubled Nate Thomas

Undercover Series
Perfect For Me
Perfect For You
Perfect For Us

Unknown Identity Series
Unknown
Unexposed
Unpublished

Standalone
Wash
Loving Charity
Summer Lovin'

Christmas Magic: A Romance Anthology
Love & College
Billionaire Heart
First Love
Frisky and Fun Romance Box Collection
Managing the Bosses Box Set #1-3

ONE WHO CAME BACK

Hades' Spawn Motorcycle Club Series

Book 3

By

Lexy Timms

ONE THAT CAME
Back
BESTSELLING AUTHOR
LEXY TIMMS

Hades' Spawn Motorcycle Club Series

One You Can't Forget
Book 1
One That Got Away
Book 2
One That Came Back
Book 3

One You Never Leave
Book 4

ONE THAT CAME
Back
LEXY TIMMS

Find Lexy Timms:

Lexy Timms Newsletter:
http://eepurl.com/9i0vD
Lexy Timms Facebook Page:
https://www.facebook.com/SavingForever
Lexy Timms Website:
http://lexytimms.wix.com/savingforever

ONE YOU CAN'T
Forget
BESTSELLING AUTHOR
LEXY TIMMS

ONE THAT CAME
Back

Description

From Best Selling Author, Lexy Timms, comes a motorcycle club romance that'll make you want to buy a Harley and fall in love all over again.

Emily Dougherty and Luke Wade were in love in high school, but circumstances conspired to keep them apart. Ten years later they meet again and find their connection is just as strong and more searingly hot than ever.

Except Luke and his motorcycle club, Hades' Spawn, are hip deep in problems between the vicious Rojos one percenter motorcycle club and their associated street gang, the Hombres. When Luke's employee and best friend, Gibs, is slain in a brutal shootout, dark secrets from Luke's past claim him. He finds he has to make a deal with the devil just to keep Emily and his club safe. However, to keep Emily out of danger he must also to turn his back on her.

Emily has lost her car, her job, and had to seek an order of protection against her ex, Evan Waters. In the face of her family's disapproval she's determined not to lose Luke too. But will Luke's heartless rejection drive her away? Or will she keep the faith and hope Luke finds his way back to her before her own secret causes her to do the unthinkable?

Can Luke and Emily survive the hopeless tangle of club and gang politics, and the fierce reach of the law to find their way back to each other?

** This is book 3 of the Hades' Spawn Motorcycle Club series **

NEW
One Christmas Night
Hades' Spawn Christmas Novella
Now Available!

Luke and Emily have each other, and their toddler son, but every other relationship in their lives is strained—the result of the violent events revolving around the Spawn and the club's president two years before.

When the president of Hades' Spawn, Oakie Walker, insists Luke and Emily host the club's Christmas Party, Luke's not very happy. Though he was reinstated as a member of the Spawn, and maintains their clubhouse, he spends only the time he has to with the club.

Emily's adoptive father, Sam Dougherty, makes no bones that biker Luke is not good enough for his daughter, while her biological father, Rob, wants to get closer to her and his grandson and no one but Emily is happy about it. Add to the mix that the president of a rival motorcycle club, the Rojos, does everything he can to create the impression that Luke will join his gang, and you have a recipe for one explosive Christmas party.

Can Luke and Emily negotiate the tricky currents of the demands from those around them? Or will it damage their relationship if they do?

NEW SERIES Coming January 2017!

EXCERPT INCLUDED!

Making Her His

Saks' Story

Anthony Parks, AKA Saks straddles two worlds and neither one is very reputable. One is as a motorcycle mechanic and Road Captain of the Hades Spawn, a none too squeaky clean motorcycle club. The other is as the scion of an organized crime family who wants him to join the family business, something he is loathed to do.

Recent events with the Spawn has soured his community reputation, and while certain women like bad boys, those kind of women are not who Saks is looking for. Add pressure from his family that "it is time to marry" Saks is faced with an impossible situation.

His wise-guy uncle proposes an arranged marriage between Saks and the daughter of a dom from another crime family. And when he meets a mysterious blonde that shows him love at first sight is possible, he knows that he could never accept his uncle proposal. Now he would just have to figure out a way to tell Uncle Vits without getting excommunicated from the family or putting the Spawn in the crosshairs of a powerful crime organization. While he is doing that he has to find the woman who has stolen his heart.

Christina

Christina Marie Serafini decided a long time ago that her loving but paternalistic family wasn't going to determine the course of her life. She had no desire to get mixed up in any of the many legal and illegal businesses her family owned. Chrissy had earned a Masters in Business and Communications on her own dime, and she just landed her dream job of Director of Marketing for an up and coming business.

Marriage and a family isn't in her game plan right now and when she did marry it was going to be a respectable man. When her grandfather announced he had arranged a marriage for her with "a nice Italian man," Christina goes ballistic. She wasn't going to marry anyone, let alone someone chosen for her. She certainly wouldn't marry a member from another crime family. Chrissy could only imagine what kind of opportunistic carogna would agree to marry a woman he never met.

Urged by her sister to at least check him out, she goes to his family's bar to confirm her suspicions. That's when she finds a handsome biker that knows exactly how to send her emotions and body into overdrive. But realizing the hunky man is the one her grandfather wants to marry sends her into flight mode evethough he haunts her dreams.

Once he finds her can Saks convince the woman of his dreams to look past his family connections to take a chance on a lowly motorcycle mechanic? And if he does, can he look past hers?

COMING January 2017

CHAPTER ONE

Deal With The Devil

Luke pushed away from the steel table of the interrogation room. *This is bullshit!* Trying to make sense of the day's events, he wanted to drive the actions of the day away forever, and another part of him wanted it engrained forever. As grief and shock washed over him, he lowered his head to his steepled fingers only to be met with a painful reminder of what happened.

Gibs was dead.

The sharp metallic scent of Gibs' blood permeated his hands. It remained even though the Witsec agent had wiped most of it away after he shoved Luke into the SUV.

Time stopped as the memory of his employee—his friend, a Hades' club member—dying beneath him swirled inside his brain. Gibs took the bullet meant for Luke. He would never erase the image of Gibs' fading eyes as he breathed his last words.

"I'm sorry," Gibs had told him. As if the man was responsible for the mess that blew up outside of his own home! As if he was the one who personally invited Sal to the place where the Rojos leader had died too.

How could Luke explain to Helen, Gibs' wife, her husband was dead or why he'd been killed? The thought weighed like lead in his stomach.

And now other Rojos were dead with Luke's name attached to their demise. Luke only knew Sal by name and reputation. Luke's association with the Rojos was short, long before the wiry Hispanic joined the outlaw motorcycle club. But Luke's rep, as the man responsible for the arrest and death of many Rojos, stuck with him even if it was undeserved. Sal, just like other of his club brothers, recognized Luke. If it weren't for the order of the imprisoned club's leader, Lil' Ricki, he would have died by a Rojos hand many years ago. Luke supposed he'd be blamed for Sal's death along with the other Hombres who died in the horrible firefight at Gibs' house.

On top of everything, another image burned into his mind. How Emily had looked at him as the police officers put her in the back of their cruiser. It crushed his heart. Fear and loss lined her beautiful face. If it wasn't for him, she'd have never been at Gibs' house, never been in the line of danger, never seen a man killed. In every way that counted, he had failed her.

He didn't know how he'd ever face her again, let alone make it up to her.

The door to the little room opened and an officer Luke hadn't seen in twenty years strode in. *Reggie*. His hair was no longer a sleek black but peppered with gray. His brown eyes, however, still had the same hard edge, of someone who had seen too much tragedy and spent his time looking for a person to pay for it.

"Well, Ray," he said in a low snarl as he took the lone seat on the opposite side of the table. "We meet again."

Luke shook his head at Reggie. "I haven't been called Ray since you took that name from me and gave me this new one." He pinched the bridge of his nose, pissed at the man, as if it was his fault Gibs had died. "This is hardly a *meeting*. That implies consent, and I did not agree for your goons to drag me away from my friend's house." The image of Gibs lying in his arms sent a shiver down his spine.

"You're the spitting image of your father, Icherra. Stubborn and stupid."

"Are we finished with reminiscing? I want to leave." Luke rose from his chair.

Reggie slammed his hand down on the metal table. It echoed off the walls and mirrored one-way glass window. "Sit down, Icherra! You think for a second! The moment your mug hits the airwaves the people your father turned in will come for your ass! There's still the matter of three million dollars missing that they count as theirs."

Two point eight thought Luke. The cops still had no idea where his dad hid that money. Luke never moved it, never touched it. Though he did check on the balance when no one could trace it. In the intervening twenty years, the money had nearly doubled. But Luke wasn't going to tell this asshole. "My problem, not yours."

The agent narrowed his eyes as he studied Luke. "Do you think you'll last more than twenty seconds out of the program now?"

Luke's breath hissed as it escaped between his teeth. "Again, *my* problem. I refuse protection. I didn't ask to enter your damn program."

"You were a kid! You didn't have a choice."

"I do now." He stared hard without blinking.

Reggie huffed and leaned back in his chair. "Okay, Icherra, I can't hold you."

"Great." Luke stood again.

"But as soon as you walk out that door the Feds are going to arrest you." Reggie didn't look up from the table. He had Luke by the balls and knew it.

"Arrest me? For what?"

"Conspiracy in a criminal enterprise."

"I had nothing to do with any of that shit! Go see Jack Kinney."

Reggie spread his hands on the table as he stood and leaned toward Luke. "Not my problem, *Spade*. You're the asshole who belongs to Hades' Spawn."

"Well, I'll take my chances."

"Sit, Icherra. I figured you wouldn't go back into the program. If you are hell bent on getting killed, then at least let's get some use out of you."

"I heart you too," sneered Luke.

"Look, asshole. Your father got my partner killed. That isn't something I'll forget. And in my book, you're the same as him."

"How would I know?" said Luke. "My parents died under your protection."

The door opened, breaking the hard stares that each man served to the other.

"Okay, Reggie. I'll take it from here."

Two men entered the room, but it was the first one, sandy-haired with blue eyes, that spoke. Reggie left with a scowl on his face. Luke looked him over. He was older than him but not by much, and skinnier. He wore a plaid shirt over a wife-beater undershirt and blue jeans. But Luke's eyes narrowed when he saw the second man, one he thought he knew well. Apparently not.

Pepper. His employee.

Fuck. This guy, the one who pleaded for a chance to work for Luke, worked for the Feds? Investigated him? Luke's eyes narrowed.

The Latino didn't look Luke in the eye. In fact, his body language, hands clenched to the side, his face tight, screamed he'd rather be any place other than here.

Luke settled back into his chair and crossed his arms.

"Mr. Wade, I'm Special Agent Leo Moyes. And this is my partner, Special Agent Hector Garcia. We work for the DEA."

"Good for you. Are you going to play good cop, bad cop? Which one is the good cop? The one that lied to me for six months?"

"I don't think you realize how much trouble you are in, Mr. Wade."

"Really? Do you care to tell me? Just what do you have on me, asshole? Did *Hector* here give a nice juicy accounting of all the *illegal* activity at my shop?"

"Luke, you know I didn't," said Hector.

Moyes glared at Hector.

"Yeah, because there isn't any. Go fucking ahead and arrest me. If the worst you got is that you don't like my friends, then prove in court I did something against the law." He held out his hands inviting them to cuff him.

"At the very least we can hold you as a material witness."

"Seriously? What makes you think that you can't secure whatever testimony I'd give you by subpoena?"

"I think you are a flight risk."

"I want to talk to my lawyer."

"You don't get a lawyer, Icherra. Or do I have to remind you your family came here illegally?"

"Are you going to treat me like an illegal alien now?"

Moyes slammed his hands down on the metal table. Did these guys have any other moves to intimidate people? Luke's eyes narrowed. Moyes didn't scare him one bit.

"If I have to, yes."

"Take a break. Let me talk to him."

Moyes shook his head, then backed away. "I'll give you five minutes." The door clicked behind the agent, leaving Luke alone with Pepper.

"So you're good cop."

"Stop, Luke. I didn't want to do this, but with Gibs' arrest we had to do something. We couldn't allow local law enforcement to blow our work. We were going to pull you in before that mess at Gibs' house. But when we requested your FBI file, Witsec was all over us."

"Somehow I'm not feeling sympathetic."

"Luke, I know you are a good guy. But people in your club are rotten to the core."

"I know it, what? What do I call you?"

"Hector is good."

"Hector, I'm not in the middle of it."

"I know that, Luke. But you got that shit going on with the Rojos. What was that about?"

"They think I'm a damn snitch. And with Witsec taking me in, they'll be even more positive."

"They disappeared before Witsec showed up, Luke."

"Makes no difference. Or did you forget a Rojos escaped? Police were at Gibs' house and they'll draw conclusions. And don't think one of those asshole Hombres weren't on the phone to their boss before they pulled the trigger."

"Look. Moyes is serious about the illegal alien shit. He'll deport you, apparently right into the hands of your not-so-loving family."

Luke looked away. He did not expect this. But Witsec giveth and Witsec could taketh away. He refused their offer of protection so all that phony identification they gave him could disappear.

"What do you want me to do, Pepp—Hector?"

"Just what you are doing, running the shop, and riding with Hades' Spawn. We can use that. The local law enforcement's harassing you to get you in deeper with Kinney." He smiled smugly. "We hold the locals back when we need to. And we'll grant you immunity from Federal prosecution."

"If what, I'm a confidential informer? A snitch?" Luke couldn't believe it. These guys had no morals. Just use, abuse and blackmail. They were their own motorcycle club, just without the wheels and a lot more guns.

"Technically, yes. But just listen to what I have to say."

Luke crossed his arms over his chest and waited. Hector wouldn't let him leave till he finished talking.

"What I—we—really want, is for you to vouch for me to patch into the club. That way I can work into Kinney's circle and get first-hand info on his operations."

Just like that? Luke wondered if the guy was losing it. "Did you see what went down at Gibs' house? Can't you do the math? The Hombres are mixed up into the Spawn! It seems there's a shake-up going down in Hombres leadership. That shit's going to blow up in everyone's faces."

"We know. We want to get it buttoned up before it gets even bloodier."

Luke sighed as he sat back in his chair. He glared at the person who was pretending to be his employee. There was no way Luke would agree. Unless... "What's in it for me?"

Hector looked at him for a long moment. "We'll get you permanent citizenship. No more threats from Witsec or immigration."

"That's a given. What else?"

Hector didn't bat an eye. He had this rehearsed to perfection. "Immunity."

"Not enough. You said immunity from Federal prosecution. I want immunity from local law enforcement too."

"I don't know if—"

"Make it happen." He stared smugly at the other man. "And there's another thing."

"Shit, what else?"

"Emily."

"Emily who?"

"The woman I've been seeing. The blonde at Gibs' house. I don't want any of this shit to touch her. No one from the government goes near her."

"We'll do what we can."

That meant no. Luke frowned. "No. You'll do it. Or the deal is off."

Hector drummed his fingers against the metal top of the table before he finally nodded. "Okay."

"And another thing. I want her local legal shit to disappear as well. She's not to face a single day in court."

Hector looked behind Luke's head to the two-way mirror glass. Luke imagined they lowered the lights in the room on the other side of the mirror so Hector could see his partner. Luke didn't bother to turn around and check.

"That's a tough one, but doable."

Luke never imagined when he made a deal with the devil, the king of hell would come in the form of a government agency. But then his father, one he barely remembered, had done the same thing twenty years ago. With a cold shiver he realized his father did it for the same reasons Luke had in mind—to protect the people he loved.

Luke was not a stupid man. He knew that every step deeper into this shit with the DEA his own life expectancy dropped more each day. He couldn't expose Emily to that same danger. That thought swathed his heart in cold so deep that what he felt for Emily, he buried as an ember sheathed in stone. She would never know what deal he had made with the devil this day – that he did it for her. He owed her. He didn't have a choice.

He loved her enough to let her go.

CHAPTER TWO

Faith

"Just where is he, Officer Anglotti?" Emily asked. The detective towered over her even though he was seated. However, she wasn't going to let him intimidate her even as tears edged the corners of her eyes. She kept her hands folded in her lap because if she didn't they would shake. It wouldn't take much more before she'd lose it altogether.

They were sitting at his desk as Emily gave her halting statement about the horrible events of that afternoon. She only did it because she figured if she cooperated he'd be more likely to give her information about Luke.

She was wrong.

"I can't say," he sneered. "Official business."

Fury rose in her and it took all she had not to swear at him. Gibs was dead! She opened her mouth, but the officer spoke before she had a chance to reply.

"I'd worry more about your own situation, Miss Dougherty." Anglotti glared at her, no doubt trying to scare her.

She wasn't afraid, but she was upset. It felt like he was attacking her, like all this was her fault. "And what would that be?" Her sight filled with tears and she didn't know how she could keep them from falling. "My situation? I've done nothing."

"Associating with a suspected drug dealer? Being involved in a fatal firefight? Any of that ring a bell?"

"What?" sputtered Emily. Raw from the events of the day, it felt as if the scowling detective had struck her. It was horrible what had happened. Men shooting at each other, Gibs killed and Luke hovering over his friend's body with such a haunted look that Emily ached for him. The sound of the gunfire had terrified her. A number of men shot. The blood. She closed her eyes briefly as the tears overwhelmed her. She blinked them open when she heard the door open.

Justin walked into the detective's office. Emily wanted to jump up and hug him.

"How'd you get in here?" Anglotti barked as he glowered at Emily's attorney.

Justin ignored the detective. "Do you have any reason to hold my client?"

"She's a witness to an event. I'm questioning her on it."

"Emily, did you give a statement?" Justin ignored Anglotti.

"Yes, Justin." She had never been so happy to see him.

"Then she's done here. Come on, Emily."

Anglotti jumped up from his chair. He jabbed a finger in Emily's direction. "Just be available for questions."

Justin stepped toward the desk and flipped his business card across it. "Contact me if you want to talk to her or I'll be talking to your chief." He spun around. "Let's go, Emily."

Emily rose. She bumped a leg of her chair and stumbled. She caught herself just before she fell. Justin looked at her with a mixture of annoyance and concern.

When they stepped into the hall with Anglotti safely out of earshot, Justin took her arm.

"Justin," Emily started.

"Not here, not now," he said tersely.

Obviously they weren't out of hearing range.

They walked down the long linoleum-lined floor. Her leather sandals slapped on the shiny floor until they reached the twin metal and glass doors. Justin pushed out into bright afternoon outside the Westfield Police Department. He led her to his car, a black Audi, and opened the passenger side door. His face was unreadable, but she sensed he was angry.

She was right.

"Just what were you doing?" he said coldly after he slipped into the car.

"Evan—"

"Evan has nothing to do with you ending up at a crime scene! It's all over the news, Emily. Men were murdered! What have I been telling you? Do you not listen to anyone? Stay away from that biker!"

She looked away, tears sliding down her cheeks.

"Em," he said more gently when he must have seen her reaction. "I can't help you if you keep ignoring my advice."

"Take me home, Justin."

"No. I'm taking you to your parents. Maybe they can talk some sense into you."

"I don't want—"

"Don't you get it?" He raised his voice and then sighed, forcibly lowering his tone. "You were at a crime scene where very dangerous men died. Dangerous. Deadly dangerous. Do you see what I'm saying? Think Emily! There are more of them! If they see your picture on the news, they could be looking for you. Do you want that?"

"I don't want them finding me. At my place or my parents' house either."

"We'll deal with that. But you are going to your parents' house." Emily's jaw set. Everything was a mess, a freaking mess! Luke's employee was dead. Poor Gibs. Now the police wouldn't tell her anything about Luke. The horrible scene replayed in her head. Men in a blue Cadillac pointing guns at the biker talking to Luke. Gibs throwing himself in front of Luke, taking the shot which was meant for Luke. The police shooting at the men in the Cadillac. Gibs on the ground and Luke on top of him. For one terrible second, she had thought Luke had been shot. She had cried out in relief when he got up.

Thankfully he got up. He was alive.

But the carnage. She didn't think she'd ever stop hearing the sounds of gunfire ripping through the air. Or the amount of bodies fallen around them. It was like a bad movie playing out in front of her.

The sound of her name startled her out of the images.

"Emily," Justin said again, apparently worried this time. "Are you okay?"

"What?" She turned her head and stared blankly at him.

"You were gone there for a couple minutes."

"Yeah," she said listlessly and sighed. Everything felt hollow inside her.

"That's it. I'm taking you to Emergency."

"No! Please don't!" Emily panicked. The last thing she wanted was to go to the hospital, especially now. "I'm okay. Just in shock." She forced a smile, but it crumbled as tears slid down her face. "They fired me, you know," she choked out. "I don't have a job. Or a car. I can't go back to my apartment. I don't know what happened to my boyfriend. I don't have anything anymore." She put her head in her hands and sobbed. She no longer cared if she sounded ridiculous.

Justin touched her shoulder briefly. "Let's get you to your parents, okay? I'll talk to them when we get there."

They drove in silence the rest of the way. When Justin opened the car door for her and helped her into the house, she let him. He led her into the living room and set her in the chair. Her parents fired questions and Justin answered what he could. She didn't argue when her mom wrapped a blanket around her. Emily sat staring blankly out the window, half listening to the conversation between Justin and her folks and mostly crying.

"She's had a bad shock," Justin explained quietly.

"And you said the police were questioning her?" her dad asked.

"Yes. I got her out, but not before she gave a statement."

Her father harrumphed. "Well, that couldn't have helped."

Emily rocked slowly in the rocking chair with the blanket around her shoulders. Why couldn't she stop crying? Even though it was a warm spring day she felt cold.

A doctor stopped by shortly after. She dimly remembered his visit, a friend of her parents' she barely knew. What's his name again? Albert... something. Albert Koos.

Why did she feel so groggy? Oh yeah, the doctor gave her a pill. She didn't like how it made her feel like she couldn't do anything. But at least she finally finished sobbing and wailing uncontrollably. By the time she stopped, her ribs were sore from hacking coughs that hit when another wave of grief crashed over her.

"Should we take her to the hospital?" asked her mother.

"No," said the doctor in his annoying doctor voice. "Not unless she tries to hurt herself. Or talks about wanting to. The girl needs rest and a couple days with minimal stress. That's a horrific ordeal she just went through. I'll write a prescription for sedatives."

"I'll get those." Her father's voice bounced loudly in the living room, strong and authoritative as always.

"One every eight hours, unless she's sleeping. Let her sleep and give it to her when she wakes."

She didn't want the pills. She wanted her brain to be clear, not in the dense fog it felt like it was hanging in now. Where was Luke? She needed him and his strong arms around her.

Then she remembered. Strange men in suits put him in an SUV and drove away. She felt like crying again, but the tears wouldn't come. She gave a long shuddering sigh. "Mom," she whispered. "I want to go to bed." She stood, her legs shaky under her. She swayed slightly.

"Sure, honey. Sam, help her."

Her father put his arm around her shoulders. "Come on. Up you go. I gotchya."

Emily stumbled as she moved across the room and up the stairs to her old room on the second floor. Her father steadied her and helped her to the room. She sat on her bed and looked around. Her parents hadn't changed much. The walls wore the same rose wallpaper she grew up with, and her white four poster bed had the rose quilt her mother made before she entered high school.

"Thanks, Dad," she said faintly. How could she feel so utterly exhausted?

"You need to lie down and sleep now. No arguments."

"But—"

He sighed loudly, cutting her off. "Fine. Is there anything you need?"

She needed Luke, but saying that wouldn't go over well. "My purse. I left it downstairs."

"Sure. I'll be right back with it. And a glass of water. You need to drink something."

Her hazy mind registered a weak protest. Sure, when Sam Dougherty got his way, with his daughter under his roof just as he wanted, he was as sweet as a puppy. But cross him and a different beast unleashed. He could have matched those Rojos anger shout for shout today.

Any other time Emily's anger would have blazed at his need to control her movements and her actions. Now it was barely an ember in her anguished heart.

Emily's head spun, and she curled up on top of the quilt. Again, she wanted to cry, especially as she pictured Luke hovering over Gibs' eerily limp body. How does it happen that one second a man lived and breathed, and the next all life was sucked from him? Her tears would not come, even as she made a face to cry them silently. They had been bled out of her body by shock and exhaustion, now leaving a hollow ache in her gut and head.

"Here, sweetie." A small weight settled at the end of the bed. A glass plinked on the wood of her old nightstand.

"Thanks, dad," she said in a small voice.

"Do you need anything else? I'll grab the paper and read it up here in your room. I told your mother to make some soup for you. She's in the kitchen now. Lucky for you, we know Dr. Koos. He doesn't do house calls anymore."

Yeah, leave me the fuck alone! If she had a scream left in her, she would have yelled it. Instead, she spoke like she always did, like a good girl. "No, thank you, daddy. I just want to sleep now."

His footsteps faded as he walked out of the room. Emily heard the familiar creak of the one step on the stairs that always protested when someone's foot hit it.

"Home," she whispered groggily and was oddly comforted by the thought. She mouthed the word again before drifting off.

Emily jerked awake several times. The medication did not help her stay asleep, or keep her awake, because each time she closed her eyes the horrible scene replayed in her mind. Yet she couldn't wake fully either because the medication kept a grip on her body and mind. She felt stuck in limbo, unable to rest or wake fully, living in a hell created by her life and fixed in place by those awful chemicals the well-meaning doctor gave her.

She shivered as a chill ran through her body. The air conditioning clicked on. Instantly a cool breeze blew over her legs and up her back. She shivered again and goosebumps prickled on her skin. There was nothing to pull over her, and she didn't have the strength to get under her quilt.

"Baby, what's wrong?"

She was sure she'd heard the question, but it couldn't be. It sounded like Luke's strong, sexy voice.

She opened her eyes and realized she was sitting in the meadow of the dream she had of her and Luke a couple days ago. Pinks and yellows streaked the sky as the afternoon sun sunk below the horizon. He sat on the grass next to her, wearing his leather jacket and reflective sunglasses. He looked so strong and beautiful she wanted nothing more than to wrap herself around him and never let go. Through her medicated haze, she was dimly aware that it wasn't real as much as she wanted it to be.

"Where are you, Luke?" she asked, hoping to get an answer from this apparition.

He pressed his hand to her heart. "I'm always here, baby. Just as you are always here for me." He took her small hand in his large one and pressed it against his jacket over his heart.

"But I don't know where you are. They took you away."

He turned his head from her. "Yes."

"You need to come back!"

He turned his head to look at her. She squinted, unable to see his eyes through the reflective lenses of his sunglasses. "This is the tough part, baby. We talked about this before."

"Before? I don't understand." She tried to remember what he meant. They'd never talked about shootings, and killings and bad guys. Never.

"Of course you don't, sweetheart. You don't remember." He looked away again. "We're never allowed to remember." His voice was sad and wistful.

She didn't understand what he was saying. It didn't make sense. She watched him stand. "Luke, don't go! I need you!" She reached for him, but he seemed just out of her grasp.

He nodded. "I need you too, but right now, you have to have faith. In us. Can you do that, baby?"

Before she could answer, he leaned in and wrapped his arms around her and took her mouth in a swift, passionate kiss. He broke from her lips and his mouth moved down. He kissed her on her breasts, tearing away the flimsy fabric of her dream dress. He left her naked and quivering under him. She worked his belt with her fingers, releasing it, and he helped pull down his jeans as he sucked hard on her nipple. Pleasure shot through her, heating her, making her want him more. She needed him inside her.

"Baby," he whispered. "I love everything about you."

Her need drove all other thoughts from her mind. "Now," she begged.

He didn't wait. He pressed the head of his shaft against her hot, wet folds and then filled her. He slid in inch by delicious inch, taking not just her body but her soul.

Her breathing sped, and she moved her hips to incite the heat which threatened to break into flame. She wanted that fire. Emily needed this man, only him. No other made her feel as he did. No other made her want to pour out all the love in her soul.

"Luke!" she cried as the universe burst apart.

His shaft pummeled her more and tore yet another orgasm from her.

"Emily!" He continued to pulse inside her, and as she came again, she knew it wasn't just his seed he gave her, but all of himself. He gave himself to her to love. To keep. To cherish. For all of time.

She woke with a start, sitting upright, suddenly awake and breathing hard. At that moment she realized she'd do what Luke had asked in the dream, to keep the faith.

Whatever happened, she loved Luke Wade too much to let him go.

CHAPTER THREE

Dancing With The Devil

Luke woke in the dark in his own apartment with his sheets wet and sticky. Through the haze of half sleep he realized he'd come in his sleep. Luke leaned back into his pillow with a soft moan. He hadn't done this since he was a teenager, but the dream of Emily was so real it shook him to his core.

They were sitting in a meadow side by side talking, and it felt peaceful there. She was so beautiful, with her blonde hair and her shining blue eyes, he had to kiss her. But in the dream they did more than that, much, much more. He took her body as she possessed his soul and they became entwined as one.

He sighed. That wouldn't happen, not ever again, which, he supposed, was why he had dreamed about her. The frustrated need he felt in high school to have her forever reared its head and roared the past few days. There were few things in Luke's life which felt right and natural. One was motorcycles. Another was his shop. But forever and always it was Emily Rose Dougherty that had first place in his heart, and he suspected would always be so.

But Luke was in too deep with the DEA's investigation of Jack Kinney to be with her. Ever again.

That, along with Gibs' death weighing on his heart, pissed him off. Mightily.

If he could, he'd pound Aces and his minions, Wolf and Dagger, into the ground. However, not only was he sworn to silence, he promised to take no action that could jeopardize the DEA's investigation.

He regretted that promise.

But tied up with his assurances that he'd play nice with the assholes responsible for Gibs' death was the DEA's agreement to Luke's price for his cooperation. Emily would be freed of local charges and no law enforcement would bother her regarding him or the shit going down in his shop or Hades' Spawn. Emily's safety and peace of mind were utmost in his mind, and with all the mayhem swirling around him, this deal was the best way he could deliver it.

Luke grabbed his iPhone from the nightstand and swiped open his messages. The sudden bright light from the display blurred his eyesight, and he rubbed his hand across his eyes. It came away damp, and he swore to himself. This was no time to lose it. There wouldn't be time for that, if at all, for many months. Image was everything now, and the tougher, the meaner, he could act would play to Jack Kinney's mercenary instincts.

Fuckin', Kinney! His instincts were basic, violent and totally self-interested. Luke intuitively understood men like Jack Kinney and was pretty sure he knew how to exploit the natural drives of men like him. He got a taste of that when he ran with the Rojos and had found it very easy to slip into their way of life. He supposed he got that from his father, his real father, not the succession of jerks who play-acted the role in his foster homes. It had taken many years before Luke pieced together his childhood recollections, colored them with the understanding of adulthood and figured the truth.

His father was a criminal.

Not a minor drug dealer, a foot soldier of a gang, or a petty thief. No, he was a major player in a Mexican drug cartel. Only he tore himself from that life to protect his wife and his young son. And it got him killed.

Like Gibs.

Luke re-swiped the screen to bring up his messages. Pepper—no Hector—he corrected himself, left a check-in message.

"Everything secure."

Luke insisted that someone stay with Helen and figured it was Hector's turn. Saks had run around all day doing errands for Luke, and Luke needed him fresh for the day. It gave Luke a small measure of satisfaction that Pepper had to play the role he was assigned as Luke's employee.

Luke never had a tougher job than confirming what Helen suspected from the news reports, that her husband was dead. The sturdy woman he knew crumpled in his arms, inconsolable in her grief. He let her cry herself out before she lay down on the bed, and the woman had a lot of tears. They left his leather jacket wet.

He now had a man's blood and a woman's tears on that jacket. That summed up his life perfectly.

It took a few days before the coroner would release Gibs' body. The waiting and uncertainty of when that would happen took a toll on Helen and, by default, Luke. He went with her to the funeral home to help her with the arrangements. He never knew there were so many details to decide, and he was relieved when Helen's sister arrived from Virginia to help. He felt both grateful and guilty he could hand off Helen's care to someone else, though he knew intellectually that her sister could help Helen in her time of grief better than he.

All he thought about was Gibs and Emily. He tried not to, but it was impossible not to.

He didn't like sitting in his apartment. His leg was on the way to healing and the most he felt was some soreness when something hit the muscle in his leg wrong. So he went to the shop and worked on the books, but even that was difficult. Everywhere he turned he thought he saw Gibs standing there, holding his coffee mug. Once, after staring for hours at his own messed-up accounting work, he dozed off. Not knowing he was asleep he stared at the image of Gibs walking into the office from the garage.

The tough old man grinned at Luke. "When?" he said, pointing to a poster on the wall. Only it wasn't a picture of a buxom blonde but Jack Kinney that straddled the Harley.

"Soon," said Luke.

"Good." Gibs strolled back into the garage.

Luke woke with a start and rubbed his eyes. Sitting here was doing no good, and he had to get the shop open soon. He resolved it would be the Monday after the funeral.

Thinking of the funeral, he went online to a florist shop and found one that personalized floral arrangements. They wouldn't make anything with a corporate name due to copyright issues, which shot down his idea of having a Harley arrangement. But they could frame a picture with flowers. Luke agreed and paid for it with his credit card, then sat back and flipped through the images on his phone to get one of Gibs. He found one of him wearing his Hades' Spawn jacket, looking over his shoulder and holding up a beer at the Red Bull. At the time, he almost ignored the impulse to take Gibs' picture, but now he was glad he'd followed through. He sent the image to the florist's shop through email.

He called Saks, and then Pepper, to announce his intention to reopen the shop. He hated calling Pepper that name now. But again, he couldn't break the cover that the agent created and Luke supposed that it would be soon enough before he'd have to sponsor Pepper for a patch.

The last thing Luke did was write a check to Helen for five thousand dollars. He didn't want her to worry about money. He was sure the five grand Gibs had taken from their savings probably put a serious dent in things, and he didn't know how Helen's financial situation was regarding her assets and Gibs' estate.

With that done he pocketed the check, and after locking up, headed for his SUV parked to the right of the building. He wanted to ride one of his bikes, but his leg was still sore.

"Wade!"

The sudden call of his name shook Luke out of his reverie. In the parking lot adjacent to his SUV, Detective Anglotti leaned against his car.

Luke shook his head, and ignored him, avoiding the cop's eyes as he walked toward his SUV.

"Hey, asshole! Talk to me."

Luke leveled his gaze to Anglotti. "On the advice of my counsel I decline to answer any questions." He opened the door of the SUV.

"Why has my investigation been shut down, Wade?" Anglotti spoke loudly, nearly shouting. His voice echoed in the early morning silence.

Luke shrugged. "Maybe because there's nothing to investigate."

"Men are dead, Wade."

Luke slammed the door shut without climbing into it. "You think I don't know that?"

"You're in the thick of it. Tell me what's going on."

Luke put on his shades, even though the sun had barely risen. "There's nothing to tell. Stop bothering me, Anglotti. I've nothing to say to you." He reopened his door and climbed into his SUV shaking with anger. The DEA promised immunity, but they didn't promise that local police would stop bothering him. In fact, they wanted it to keep Luke's evolving cover as a loyal Hades' Spawn member willing to move up.

He hated this. This wasn't him. It wasn't the man he wanted to be.

But he had to. For Emily's sake. "Dammit!"

He pulled out of the parking lot and headed away from Anglotti. Not sure where to go, he drove for a while before finally stopping by Gibs' house.

Helen's sister, Mary, answered the door. "Hello, Luke. She's finally sleeping."

"That's good. Can you give this to her? Tell her it was the bonus I was supposed to give Frank."

Mary took the check and her eyes narrowed.

"This isn't a bonus check," she said. "It's made out to Helen."

"I want her to have it. I know things will be tough. Nothing'll make up for Frank's loss, but I don't want her struggling financially also."

Mary handed him the check back. "We Andersons don't take charity."

He shoved his hands in his jean pockets. "I'm not taking it back. If she doesn't cash it, I'll just send her another one." He leaned forward and whispered in her ear. "I can be stubborn too. And I know where she lives." He purposely kept his tone light.

Mary smiled. "Okay, Luke. I'll give it to her. But you can expect much the same response."

"All I can do is try. Has anyone else from the club been by?"

Mary shook her head. "Only Saks and Pepper. They come by regularly to check up on us."

Luke nodded, feeling a slow burn. "Well, everyone in the club will be at the funeral."

"I'm sure." She said it politely, but not understanding the importance of the club's loyalty.

"I'll see you later then." Luke got into his SUV feeling his anger roiling in his stomach. Kinney caused Gibs' death and didn't have the decency to pay his respects to Helen? It was outrageous. What else could he expect from a coward? Aces sent Gibs to do his dirty work and dragged him into the middle of the Rojos and the Hombres. Luke ground his teeth as he drove away.

It didn't take him long to reach the Red Bull. He scanned the lines of motorcycles and found Aces, Wolf, and Dagger's bikes parked together.

He thought a few moments, trying to decide what he wanted to do. The angry part of him wanted to call out Kinney and give him a good beating. The calculating part of him wanted to reel the f'er in and let him get spit roasted slowly by the burn of his crimes. His brain won out over his heart this time. Beating up Kinney would provide a moment's satisfaction. Watching him get thrown in jail for twenty years would provide years of revenge.

Luke pasted a smile on his face and entered the bar. He scanned the room and found Kinney's table. With a motion of his hand, he indicated to John, the barkeeper, to send a round to the table. John knew enough what Luke liked to drink so it arrived with the others after Luke sat down.

"Hey guys," he said.

"Luke!" Kinney blinked in surprise. "What brings you here?"

Luke took a sip of his beer and looked Kinney in the eye. It was nearly lunch... nearly. Or it had to be five o'clock somewhere. "Too bad about Gibs. I hear he was helping you out."

Kinney settled back in his seat and stared at him, as if trying to gauge Luke's comment and the man himself.

"Everyone helps his brothers in the club."

"Not this kind of help."

Kinney glanced at Wolf, then Dagger, who both crossed their arms over their chests and sent Luke hard stares from their tough faces.

"So what of it?" Kinney shrugged and smiled.

"I'm a businessman, Aces. I believe I've shown I have connections."

"That Rojos president is dead."

"You don't think I know that?" Luke fired back each of his responses as if he'd rehearsed them. "You think that matters? And you think he was the only connection I have?"

Kinney sniffed and rubbed his nose.

From Kinney's reactions to his comments, Luke surmised the depth of Aces' stupidity. The man used his own product. That made this club's president both easier and more difficult to deal with. It might be easier to get in with him because his judgment was clouded, but the man would be more paranoid and unpredictable. Luke sighed, pretending to give in. "Fine. Then let's talk business." Luke took another sip of his beer. He'd dance with the devil if it meant avenging Gibs' death, and right now that devil was Jack Kinney.

CHAPTER FOUR

Luke's Letter

The next number of days went by in a haze for Emily. Somehow, in her drug influenced mind, she knew that taking the medicine was doing her no good. Sure, she slept, but her dreams were disturbed and she hated being suspended between waking and sleep. The next morning, when her mother brought the pills, she refused to take them. She wanted her mind back, not the drugged one. Towards the end of the day, she began to feel more like herself.

Somehow during the ensuing days of haziness, her clothes were shed, and she'd been wearing one of her mother's terrycloth bathrobes. On the chair under the window, her clothes sat neatly folded. She brought them to her nose, confirming her suspicion that they had been freshly laundered.

After taking a shower, she dressed and made her way down the stairs following the scent of warm cooked food. Her mother and father were in the dining room seated at the table.

"Emily!" Her mother stared at her in surprise.

"Hi, Mom." She gave her a kiss on the cheek, then rounded the table and did the same for her dad.

"How're you feeling?" he asked.

"Tired. But I can't sleep my life away so I don't have to deal with reality."

"Sit, I'll bring you a plate." Her mother disappeared into the kitchen, returning a moment later carrying a plate of meatloaf with gravy, mashed potatoes, and peas.

Emily smiled. It must be Wednesday. That was her mother's meatloaf day. "Looks great, Mom. Thanks."

"What do you want to drink?"

"Iced tea?"

"Sure."

Her mother hurried back to the kitchen as her father cleared his throat. "I'm glad you're finally up. Justin called. He said he had some news."

"What kind of news?"

"He didn't say. Just said he wanted to talk to you."

"Oh." She wondered if Justin had told her dad and he just didn't wish to say anything, like a silly control thing. Or maybe he simply didn't know. She shouldn't jump to conclusions without asking.

Her mother brought the iced tea and sat back down. Emily waiting for them to say grace then realized they must have already done it. She tried a bite and nearly moaned with how good it tasted in her mouth.

They continued to eat in stilted silence, as if they were afraid to say anything to upset her.

It began to get annoying. She knew she'd been a burden the past few days but she wasn't a leaf petal, she wasn't as fragile as they thought she was. If they only knew... She shook her head to clear the thoughts and images running through her mind. "Good meatloaf, mom. Did you change the recipe?"

Her mother gave a little shrug. "Justin's mom has a different take on meatloaf. She mixes in ground pork and uses this garlic and herb blend of breadcrumbs. Your father liked it very much when we had dinner at her house last week."

Her father's cheeks colored. "I was just being polite, Amanda."

Emily nearly laughed out loud. *Well, this is interesting.* Sam Dougherty had never liked another person's cooking over his wife's in his life. Even restaurant food paled in comparison to Amanda Dougherty's culinary skill. This odd bit of tension over something so mundane was almost funny, it was so precious. Then Emily thought of something else.

"Wait a sec," Emily said, catching the whiff of a conspiracy. "Why'd you eat at Justin's mom's house?"

Her father muttered something like 'done in by meatloaf" and her mother blushed. They both went back to their food, stuffing large bites of meatloaf inside their mouths to save them from having to answer.

Their actions were entirely visible. Emily bit back a smile and a head of annoyance. "Come on. Out with it."

"Oh dear." Her mother covered her mouth and her eyes grew big. "We weren't supposed to say."

"They wanted," said her father gravely, "to wait for the Memorial Day picnic to make the announcement." He acted as if Emily had uncovered some ancient secret no one was supposed to know.

"Announcement? Are they...?"

"Yes." Her mom nodded. "They're getting married."

An image of Luke and her in front of a priest saying vows popped into her head. Blinking heavily she pushed it away. "That's wonderful." And then another thought hit her. "Why didn't Angela tell me herself?"

"You've had a lot of things on your plate, dear." Her mom patted her hand. "She didn't want to—"

"Oh, for heaven's friggin' sake! I'm not a broken doll! I have the capacity to be happy for my sister even if my life feels like shit."

"Emily!" Her mother's mouth popped open and her eyebrows disappeared behind her curled bangs.

"Language!" warned her father.

"Language?" said Emily indignantly. "I've heard you use that word a few times, Dad. And while we're at it, I'd appreciate it very much if you didn't treat me like I was going to break at any second. I'm not the fuck-up you all think I am."

Her mother's face turned bright red.

"Emily!" Her father shouted and then muttered, "That stupid Wade boy."

"This is not about Luke!" She glared at her father.

He stood and fumed. "You know what? I don't give a pig's eye what you think this is about! You act like you are all high and mighty and know better than anyone! You ignore our advice and when things go all wrong, you cry that you've been treated unkindly. You still don't listen to your parents! And when the shit hits the fan, and it always does when you're around Emily, you come crawling back here expecting us to be all understanding and forgiving. You put your mother through hell these past few days!"

Emily opened her mouth to shoot a retort back at him and then pressed it firmly shut as she clenched her jaw. He always had to be so friggin' unreasonable! He—

"Hey, hey, what's all this?"

All eyes turned as Justin spoke from the entrance of the dining room. Still in shock, Emily realized Justin's status in the family had changed. He felt comfortable walking into the house without knocking.

"Sorry, son," said her father. He stood and shook Justin's hand. "Everything's fine here. But unfortunately, the secret's out. Can't keep anything from a Dougherty woman. She'll scope it out, even if your heart's slowly stopping." He shot a look of warning at Emily, as if daring her to say more.

"That's okay," said Justin with a smile. "Angela's been dying to tell Emily." He coughed. "I mean, she's been anxious to let you know." Justin leaned toward his future father-in-law, a teasing smirk on his lips. "I understand there's a lot of super-secret girl stuff that goes on before a wedding. Highly top secret."

Her father rolled his eyes. "I suppose."

"You look better Emily." Justin took a seat opposite her at the table. "I have some good news."

"Would you like anything?" Emily's mom got up, ready to make a plate of food for him.

Justin waved his hand. "I'm fine, thank you. I'm on my way home now. I won't be here long. I want to catch up with Angela before she heads into work."

"So what's the good news?" Emily suddenly wanted something to look forward to, anything to get her out of the house.

Justin shook his head. "It's crazy. All the charges against you have been dropped."

"That's wonderful," enthused her mother.

"How?" Emily stared at him, trying to process what he meant. "Why?"

Justin smiled, pleased to have surprised her. "The DA said he looked over the case. Apparently, with the little evidence there was, it was easy to see that Evan was trying to make your life difficult. He's dropped the theft charges, and because of what he termed 'an overzealousness to prosecute' dropped the traffic charges as well."

"Isn't that unusual?" For all the stress and anxiety she'd been through the past while, it didn't seem like the case would be dropped that easily. "It's all dropped? Just like that?"

"Just like that." Justin laughed. "I'm not going to question our good fortune. Neither should you." Justin stared at her, his eyebrows raised. "Hey! Be happy, Emily. We won!"

Emily could easily imagine why Justin would be happy. With this miraculous 'win' he'd look like a legal god to his employers. She knew she sounded bitter inside her head. Her father's outburst a moment ago continued to stew in her mind. It seemed to take the tarnish off of what should feel good. She also missed Luke. She wanted to know where he was and if he was okay. She forced a smile. "I am glad. Sorry, if I don't show it." She rubbed her forehead. "I think I'm just still groggy from the anti-anxiety pills." Or whatever they were.

Justin stood. "Now be ready at eight sharp Monday morning. I'll pick you up for your hearing on the restraining order against Evan. While we're at it, we'll get back your bail money."

"Aren't you going to be here for Sunday dinner?" Emily's mother suddenly came back to life.

"Of course." He winked. "Wouldn't miss it." He kissed his mother-in-law-to-be's cheek and slapped Emily's father's shoulder on his way out.

"Good night, son," said Sam Dougherty warmly. He walked Justin to the door.

Seeing how her father was with Justin made Emily's heart sink. He apparently thought of Justin as a son—the son he always wanted. She was happy for Justin, but at the same time knew that Luke would never measure up to those standards. He hadn't back in high school and he never would now, even with a successful business and real life. Luke didn't stand a chance. Maybe they didn't stand a chance.

With her father out of the room, Emily carried her half empty plate to the kitchen and told her mother she was going to bed early. She faked being exhausted and headed back upstairs.

Emily woke the next day before her parents were up. She checked her phone, just like she had checked it a hundred times the previous night. There was still no message from Luke. She was worried. It had been days and he hadn't made any effort to contact her. She wanted to know how Helen was doing but didn't have Gibs' number, and Luke hadn't replied to her texts.

She sighed, frustrated already and not even out of bed yet. Her phone beeped, warning her that the charge was low.

Had Luke been arrested that day? What happened? Emily used what precious battery was left on her phone to do a Google search, trying to find a news report or a follow-up, but there wasn't much information. She found one article on the shooting.

Gang Violence Hits Westfield

Five unidentified victims lost their lives in a shoot-out on the residential street of Carmel Street Friday evening. Police have given no details, citing this incident as an ongoing investigation. Neighbors identified one victim as Francis Gibson, a long-time resident of Westfield. They called him a quiet man who was friendly with his neighbors.

"We never expected anything like this," said Olson Cooper of Carmel Street. "And certainly not from Frank. Sure, he drove a motorcycle, but he was a motorcycle mechanic so you'd expect that. I feel for his wife. She's a lovely woman."

Neighbors also report seeing motorbike riders wearing gang colors, but couldn't identify which one.

According to neighbors' reports, the scene was cleared before midnight after many police officers cordoned off and investigated the scene.

Using Gibs' full name, Emily did another Internet search and found his obituary, which led to a memorial page put up by the funeral home. Tears ran down her face as she read the poignant remembrances of a man well-loved by those who knew him.

Emily read them all but didn't find one from Luke. It worried her. If anything, Luke would put up a memorial to his employee and friend, right? Unless he wasn't able to because he was in jail or been dragged away somewhere. She went to send him another text and her phone battery died just as she started typing.

The visiting hours for Gibs were this evening and Emily resolved to go.

But first she needed to get out of this house.

She heard her mother stirring in the hallway and then the close of the bathroom door. Shortly after, her mother descended the stairs, the creak of the old steps marking her passage.

Emily rose from her bed and began pacing. She needed to go home and change. She had no dress clothes or anything appropriate to wear here at her parents' house.

The doorbell rang, and Emily flew to the window to see who it was.

Her heart sped when she spotted a motorcycle in the street. Squinting, she realized it wasn't Luke's and the crush of disappointment made her want to cry.

Forcing the silly tears away, she hurried down the stairs, realizing it was Saks' bike. *Speak of the devil.* "I'll get it, Mom," she called out quickly.

Emily was at the door before her mother could travel the length from the kitchen to the living room.

"Saks!" She hugged the big lug tightly, so incredibly happy to see him.

"Hey, Emily!" Saks chuckled and unwrapped her arms from around his neck. "I brought your overnight bag." He handed it to her.

"You're a life saver." The timing couldn't be more perfect. "Have you—"

"Emily, who is it?"

Emily rolled her eyes at Saks, feeling like she was fifteen all over again. "It's for me, Mom," she called to the living room.

Saks' eyebrows went up. "What are you doing here?"

She waved her hand. "Long story. How'd you know I was here? Never mind." She didn't honestly care, she was just happy to see him. "Have you heard from Luke? I hope he's okay."

Saks looked perplexed. "Luke's fine, Emily."

"He is?" She couldn't keep the disappointment from her voice. "I hadn't heard from him at all. I've tried to mess..." She knew she sounded lame. "My phone's dead. I need to recharge it." She knew she was babbling, but the sudden nervous butterflies in her stomach threw her off.

"Things are a mess since... since Gibs'... you know." Saks was clearly uncomfortable with the conversation. "There's a note from Luke in the bag." He ran a hand through his hair and glanced around. "Catholic, 'eh?" He sighed and blinked suddenly before clearing his throat. "Look, I've got to go. I'm sorry, Emily."

"It's okay," she started to say, but Saks spun and stepped quickly out of the house.

"Later, Emily."

"Sure, Saks. Thanks," she told his quickly retreating figure. She had a good feeling he hadn't even heard her. He looked like he was in a rush to get back on his bike.

Saks drove off without even a wave or acknowledgement. Emily hurried back inside and shut the door.

"Who was that, Em?"

Flippin' eh? Did her mother have to eavesdrop on everything? Wiping a tear she didn't even know had fallen from her cheek with the back of her hand, she said, "Just a friend returning something." She pulled the bag she'd packed last Friday over her shoulder.

"All right. I could have sworn I heard a man's voice."

You did, Mom. She bit her lip to stop the reply from sneaking out.

"So what do you want for breakfast tomorrow morning? Scrambled? If you want eggs I have to go and get some. Or ask your father."

Trust her mom to think of food when Emily felt like her whole life was falling apart. "Whatever's fine. Whatever's easiest for you." She turned to head up the stairs.

Her mom came around from the living room and leaned against the frame. She studied Emily as if trying to read her. "Are you feeling okay?"

"Yeah." Emily nodded. "I'll get dressed" She hurried up the stairs, not waiting for her mother to reply. Back in her room she unzipped the bag with shaking hands. She desperately wanted Luke's note.

She drew out the plain envelope with her name written on it in Luke's plain block lettering. It took her a moment before she opened it, suddenly unsure if she actually wanted to read what he had to say.

Finally, she broke and unsealed the glued edge with her fingernail. Her stomach grew strangely queasy. Somehow she knew the letter would ruin everything.

She hesitated on the first word Luke had scribbled down. Emily.

Something was wrong. Tears filled her eyes. She didn't want to read the letter. If she put it away and pretended she never saw it, would it allow things to stay the same? A loud sigh slipped from her mouth. Everything had changed.

Emily,

These are tough words because I never meant to hurt you. You saw some awful things about me, things I never meant for you to see. But the fact remains that I'm no good for you. A good woman like you deserves better, much, much better.

I know how you'd like to argue with me, and tell me I'm not the kind of man you saw last Friday, but it wouldn't be true. It would just be the illusion I wanted you to see, that I'm a good person.

I am not.

Emily, you deserve more than to be saddled with a criminal, and that's what I am. Men like me end up dead, like Gibs. I have no illusions about that. You don't deserve to cry over my grave like Helen is for Gibs.

Don't try to call me again. I won't take your call. Don't try to see me again. I won't talk to you.

Save yourself from heartache and forget about me. Find yourself a man that's worthy of you. We shared some great moments together, but that's all it was.

Goodbye,

Luke

Emily blinked as tears rolled down her cheeks, blurring the words she stared at. The letter was so cold, so deliberately cruel. How could he do this? How could he underestimate their relationship just like her parents did? Did he think she'd turn tail and run when things got unpleasant or a little rough?

Maybe she deserved that. That's exactly what she did when her parents pressured her in high school. She dropped him and ran off to California. Maybe this was payback. He'd played her all along, stringing her into liking him and everything.

She clenched her jaw. *Screw him! No, wait! Fuck him!*

Well, she was done running. Maybe it took a while for it to sink into her thick Irish head, but she loved Luke and she knew to her deepest core that he loved her. And if Luke Wade thought she was that easy to get rid of, he had another thing coming.

CHAPTER FIVE

Calling Hours (Luke)

Luke stepped out of his SUV dressed in a new suit he bought for Gibs' funeral. He'd never owned a suit before and thought it was an incredibly bad omen that the first one he bought was for one of the saddest events in his life. Would he be wearing it again, for his own funeral?

In the movies, it rains on funerals, the dark atmosphere complementing the sadness of the scene. But on this day, it was a bright and sunny spring day, neither too hot nor too cold. A New England rarity. Days like this happened maybe seven days out of the entire year.

The sky seemed to be mocking Luke's sadness.

He came early because Helen asked him to.

Saks and Pepper would be close behind. He made sure they checked the shop and headed over. One of the funeral staff opened the double doors to let him in, and he saw the placard with Gibs' name on a table to the left, just before a wide entrance to the viewing room.

He was assaulted by the smell of flowers. The sweet, spicy, peppery scent of carnations dueled with the stronger, almost sickly sweet smell of lilies. He sucked in a long breath and held it as he stepped inside the room. He walked past the photo board, not sure he could take looking at it. What was ahead was worse. Gibs laid out in his coffin in the repose of death, the many flowers sent by family and friends framing the coffin.

Luke walked straight to Helen and her sister and gave them each a hug. "I'm so sorry," he whispered.

Helen pressed her hand against his. "Thank you for coming," she said, totally ignoring his admission of guilt. He had told her he was sorry before, but she refused to accept that Luke was the cause of her husband's death.

"Frank thought the world of you, you know. If we had a son, he'd want him to be like you."

Luke patted her back, struggling to hold back the riot of emotions that threatened to break him. In the back of his mind, he had thought of Gibs as the father he never really had. Their employer-employee relationship stifled most of that, but out of all the other men who worked for Luke, it was Gibs who he relied on. Always.

Helen took Luke's hand and walked with him to the casket. She knelt, and touched Gibs' arm, stroking it.

Luke swallowed hard. It burned his throat and heart to watch the loving touches of this woman for her deceased husband. It was as if she was trying to comfort him even in death.

He stood rigidly behind her, holding his hands in front and then he helped Helen stand when they heard the first people walk into the room.

"Thank you, Luke." She walked back to the row of Queen Anne chairs set up for the family.

Luke drifted off to the far corner of the room near the front of the funeral home. He leaned against the wall as he watched people come in. Helen greeted some people, and a few sat down in the chairs. Luke didn't know any of them.

Helen looked around the room and found him, waving Luke over to the group. She made introductions, all from her side of the family. Helen explained that Gibs had one brother, but they had a falling out years ago, so she didn't expect to see him.

Her story nearly drove him to tears. Over the years, he had wished for a family to call his own, and if he had a brother, he'd never let any argument get between them.

Friends and neighbors of the couple arrived and offered their condolences to Helen and her family. Finally Saks, then Pepper, came. Saks, like Luke, wore a suit, but Pepper just wore a button down and some jeans. They said a few words to Helen and offered condolences to the family. Luke walked over to the photo board and they followed, all gazing at the pictures of Gibs' life.

There were pictures from all parts of his life, from when he was a boy with his parents and brother to current ones at the shop and on rides. Saks pointed to the image of Gibs at a barbecue at his house, and to some photos of Gibs on his bike amid a crowd of other club members. "I remember that," he said quietly.

As they gazed at the photos Ace, Wolf and Dagger in tow, came through the funeral home. Some other men Luke didn't recognize, wearing club jackets, came through as well.

"Hey, Spade," said Kinney, looking up and down at Luke's suit.

"Ace." He nodded to Wolf and Dagger.

"These are some brothers from Tucson. Cord, Mex, Joker and Rocker."

Luke looked over at the men. He didn't like what he saw. Under their open jackets, they wore their leather cuts, one percent and number thirteen diamonds and various colors of wings flashing as they moved. They were unshaven and grungy. You didn't come to a funeral underdressed and dirty. You represented the club. Always.

"Helen's over there," Luke pointed, keeping his voice in check.

"Yeah, I see. Boys, let's go pay respects to Gibs' old lady."

Luke cringed. Though the term 'old lady' was used in many gangs for the wife or permanent girlfriend of a club member. Hades' Spawn members weren't that militant. But what he saw when they walked toward her nearly caused him to rush over and start a fight. He looked away for a moment, not sure what to do, and to calm his anger.

"Luke, you see that?" asked Saks incredulously, elbowing Luke.

"He isn't wasting any time, is he?" Pepper cast an appraising law enforcement eye on the spectacle.

It wasn't about Ace hitting on Helen. Though Luke wouldn't have put it past the asshole, it was worse. The men wore their colors on the back of their leather jackets. While the center colors were the same as Luke's jacket, an elaborate skull sitting on top of a pair of wings, they sported the club name in a top rocker, a patch in the shape of an arch over the picture, and a bottom rocker with the territory of the club scribed inside.

Luke shook his head. He should have been expecting this. Okie had warned him in his letter about the Tucson club. However, it wasn't just the Tucson club. What made him stare was Aces' jacket. It wasn't the one piece patch of their local chapter. Theirs had the name above the colors typical of a social motorbike club with no territory listed. No, Aces' patch sported a top rocker like the Tucson crew. Adding insult to injury, he had a bottom rocker with the declaration "Connecticut".

Like most everything else in club life, patches or "colors" were strictly codified. A social club like the Spawn local would have one or sometimes a two-piece patch. Only outlaw gangs like the Rojos wore the three-piece patch.

"Fuck," muttered Luke under his breath. This would only piss off the Rojos. It was, in effect, a declaration of war by claiming Rojos territory for Hades' Spawn.

"He really wants to get us killed, doesn't he?" said Luke, only loud enough for Saks and Pepper to hear.

Saks muttered and shook his head. "This shit needs to stop, or I'm out of the club. This is insane."

Luke agreed in his heart, but as Pepper studied his reaction, he knew he had to play the role he signed on for. "I'm not leadership." He shrugged.

"Well, maybe you should be. Look, I'm outta here. I'll be at the Red Bull. Later."

Luke remembered that Saks had mentioned he was cousins with the owner, Rocco, and his brother John of the Red Bull. Saks probably wanted to warn them of the impending trouble.

He couldn't blame Saks.

Other members of the club entered, most with their wives or girlfriends. Nearly every one of them wore suits or regular street clothes. The men stared incredulously at Aces and the Tucson crew.

"What's going on, Spade?" said Spider, otherwise known as Henry Spinner.

"Aces has visitors."

Spider's eyes narrowed watching the knot of unkempt men now standing in front of the photo board.

"Those jackets."

"Yeah," said Luke.

"Okie should have told us."

Again, Luke didn't disagree, but with Pepper watching him, he couldn't express that sentiment.

"I like the look of those jackets," said Pepper.

Spider's face fell before he shot the back of Aces' jacket a look of disgust. "Yeah," he said, his lips curling up. "Because being a criminal is so damn cool."

"Oh, Luke," a familiar soft voice cried behind him.

Luke closed his eyes briefly before he turned. He did not need this.

Deirdre, his girlfriend from earlier in the year, stood dressed in a black sheath, and for once, black stilettos. She looked beautiful, as always, which is what drew him to her in the first place. She threw her arms around his neck and kissed his cheek.

"Hello, Deirdre. Sweet of you to come." Even he heard the chill in his voice. The last thing he needed was his ex-girlfriend's theatrics in the funeral home.

"Of course! I had to come."

"That's Gibs' wife right there. Her name is Helen." But before he could extricate Deirdre from his arm, another woman walked through the entrance.

Oh, for fuck's sake.

"Hi, Luke. How's the leg?" Sheila wore a black skirt and matching blouse. She was dressed a hundred times more decent than Deirdre, except for the amount of buttons done up at the top of her blouse.

"It's fine, Sheila." Luke ignored Spider's chuckle beside him. He motioned to both ladies. "Sheila, this is Deirdre."

"Oh! I remember you from high school. Sheila Harmon, right? You were a couple years ahead of me."

"Yes, but it's Healey now."

"Oh, you're married." Deirdre's scowl brightened to a smile.

"*Was*." Sheila studied the woman hanging onto Luke. Her eyes traveled up and down, as if assessing an enemy.

"Oh." Deirdre probably had a hundred different ways to say that word. She had that look in her eye that Luke knew well. The woman was about to explode. "What's up with your leg, Luke?" The words slid out of Deirdre's mouth like a snake hissing a warning.

"Just a little accident," said Sheila brightly, concluding that Deirdre was not part of Luke's recent life. "I helped him with his dressings." Sheila spoke in a seductive tone that colored the meaning of the words.

Luke swallowed. The thought crossed his mind that he needn't worry about gang violence if he didn't make it out of the funeral home alive. He glanced at Helen, hoping she couldn't hear this ridiculous conversation going on. A movement by the door caught his attention and he gasped.

His reaction had Spider looking over and chuckling. "*Another* one?"

At the entrance stood Emily, dressed in a very sensible dark two-piece suit. The look on her face as her eyes moved toward him, crushed him. Taking a moment to gather herself, she straightened and raised her chin.

She solemnly walked past him, both ladies beside him watching her with their mouths hanging open. Emily knelt in front of Gibs' coffin and crossed herself before bending her head in prayer. After a minute, she made the sign of the cross again and stood to talk to Helen. She laid an envelope down on a table set up next to the coffin, then moved towards Gibs' family. She spoke quietly with Helen, gave her a hug and then moved down the line of relatives expressing her condolences. She was a class act – proper, classy and sophisticated. Luke felt a swell of pride, even though he was furious with her for coming. She should have stayed away, kept herself safe.

"Hey," said Deirdre, using a finger to pull Luke's head back toward her. "Just what's going on here?"

CHAPTER SIX

Calling Hours (Emily)

Emily was never as nervous as when she pulled in the parking lot of the funeral home. Her stomach fluttered, and she felt the annoying queasy feeling that seemed to becoming part of her daily routine. But if Luke was anywhere, he'd be here.

She wasn't fooling herself by trying to conjure the lie that she was here to honor the man she saw shot in front of her. That was the valid reason for being here. However, the truth was she wanted to see Luke and force him to see her.

She wanted answers.

It may very well be true that Luke thought he wasn't good enough for her. He always had an edge of self-deprecation, though he didn't share that with the world. She didn't care. Still, knowing him since high school, she sensed there was something behind that tough-man facade that haunted him. He had hinted at it himself:

"I did get into trouble. It was bad. I thought I got into trouble because after you left I had nothing to live for. But, looking at it now, I'd have done it whether you were there or not."

Emily swallowed hard and screwed up her courage to walk the distance to the doors of the funeral home. Once inside, she found the showing room and stepped through the wide entrance and then stopped short.

Ahead of her stood Luke, looking damnably sexy in a dark suit. That part caught her breath, but the two women overdressed in ridiculously sexy outfits for a funeral standing on either side of him burned anger into her blood. One of them clung to his arm. The other was Sheila Harmon.

Doing a slow burn, she walked past him, arching an eyebrow at him briefly, then made her way to Gibs' coffin. She looked at the man in the stillness and chill of death. Gibs only seemed to be asleep, but she knew he would never wake. She sunk to her knees and said a prayer for him, hoping that his stay in purgatory would be short and he could join his Father in heaven soon.

A lifelong Catholic, Emily knew all souls not condemned to hell spent some time in purgatory atoning for their earthly sins. She rose and placed the Mass card she got from Father Peters this morning on the table for the sympathy cards. Sometime in the next month, Father Peters would dedicate a mass for Gibs' soul, to help ease his entrance into heaven. Father Peters was kind, knowing of Emily's recent troubles, and wouldn't take a large donation for the mass, for which Emily was grateful. It was a small thing, but something Emily felt she should do. While she was at the church, she also lit a candle for Gibs and said a prayer for him.

She also lit a candle for her and Luke and instead of the usual Hail Mary or Our Father, put her prayer in her own words.

Heavenly Father,

I know in your wisdom you brought Luke and me together, but it seems everyone wants to keep us apart. Help me find a way to understand what You want for us. Amen.

Emily was amazed at the grace which Helen handled these calling hours. The woman greeted each person and hugged them, thanking them for coming. Emily knew if it were her, she'd be a puddle of tears throughout the whole affair.

"Thank you for coming." Helen's words were automatic until she realized who she was speaking to. Her eyes grew big and filled with tears that didn't fall. "Emily." Helen tried to smile.

"I'm so sorry," Emily whispered, feeling tears in her eyes again.

"You were there," Helen whispered.

"Yes," Emily mouthed, barely able to speak now. She nodded.

Helen leaned over and whispered in her ear. "Tell me it was quick. Tell me he felt no pain."

Emily's shoulders shook. She tried to block out the images in her head but they refused to leave. "He saved Luke's life," she choked out. She wiped her eyes, embarrassed by the tears and her voice shaking.

Helen shot a quick look at Luke, then back at Emily. She put her hands on Emily's arms. "Frank looked hard and tough, but inside he was entirely unselfish. That's why I love..." She bit her lip. "That's why I loved him."

"You were lucky to have each other." Emily's tears now slid like a river down her cheeks.

"Here," said Helen, taking some tissue from a box on the floor by her chair. "The funeral home put out a generous supply." She handed a Kleenex to Emily then dabbed at her own eyes. "Please drop by the house after the funeral. I'd like to speak with you."

Emily hesitated, unsure if she could ever go by that street again.

Helen squeezed her arm. "Please?"

"Yes, of course." Emily wiped her eyes. "I will. Thank you." She moved to the next relative, then the next, offering her condolences. With the juggernaut of her emotions hitting her at once, it felt like she was moving in slow motion as she spoke to each one. She struggled with her tears and managed to gain control and contain them, though her heart felt like it would burst. She felt so guilty. She should be thinking about Helen and what she was going through, not about the silly boy behind her.

She refused to turn her head and look at Luke. She felt he was watching her but she made herself ignore him. The full possibility that she lost Luke forever hit her like an arrow piercing her heart. Helen's grief over losing her husband, Luke standing there with two women flanking him, drove home the point he might be beyond recovering.

She couldn't stand the thought. The anger that had boiled not long ago returned. She blinked several times. Women were crazy–she was one of them. They could blow through emotions faster than the wind blew a sail. She forced air through her nose and let the anger replace the sadness.

Luke was hers. That was all there was to it.

When she reached the end of the receiving line, she brought her eyes to Luke. The woman she didn't recognize had her fingers on Luke's jaw. She looked familiar, but Emily couldn't remember who she was. Darn thing about small towns. Everyone knew everybody and everyone looked slightly familiar. Didn't matter, she'd had enough.

That's it! Emily marched over to Luke and the two women.

"Emily!" Sheila smiled a little too brightly. "It's good to see you. Well, not under the circumstances, but still good to see you."

"Whatever," hissed Emily. A fire had lit under her and she had no intention of playing the good girl now. Where did it get her? *Nowhere!* "Luke, I need to speak to you. Privately." She kept her tone even, but made it clear she wouldn't take no for an answer.

"Excuse me." Luke plucked Deirdre's arm off his. He smiled weakly at a laughing Spider and followed Emily.

She marched out of the room, looking around for somewhere private to talk. A staircase leading to a second floor barred by a chain strung between the wall and banister. She unhooked the chain and handed the end to Luke.

"Emily," he said.

She shook her head and crooked it to point up the stairs. Luke sighed and followed her, replacing the chain as he stepped on the stairs.

Silent, Emily hurried up, knowing Luke was following at a slower pace behind her. *Tough shit! He wants to act like a dog with his tail between his legs, let him!* All the stress and terror of the past few days—screw that—from the past few weeks turned into anger, all pointed at Luke.

At the top of the stairs was a long hallway with doors. Emily tried each handle until she found one that was unlocked. She stepped inside. It was an office with a large antique oak desk to the right and a large full bookcase behind it. A few other chairs spread across the room.

Luke followed her in with a cold look on his face. He shut the door behind him quietly. "What do you want, Emily?" His face was unreadable.

"You need to explain this." She pulled Luke's letter from her pocket.

He slipped his hands in his pockets. "There isn't anything to tell. I meant what I wrote."

Emily's lip quivered, and she cursed herself for coming close to losing it again. No. Not after everything they shared. Her anger rose and pushed out the next words she spoke. "No." She lifted her chin stubbornly. "I don't believe a word of it."

Luke sighed. "I knew you wouldn't. That's why I sent the letter, to avoid a scene like this." He turned to open the door.

No! He was not getting away that easy. She wasn't going to let him do this to her. "Wait!"

He turned back, his face a mirage of emotions. He pressed his lips together before his shoulders dropped. He looked incredibly handsome and vulnerable. It was a side of him she had never seen. "This isn't going to do us any good," he said quietly. He blinked and pressed his emotions away before straightening.

Emily stepped forward and put her hand on his arm. "Luke, don't do this. I love you."

His eyes flashed. Whatever vulnerability was there a moment ago disappeared. Emily almost drew back from the anger she saw replacing it.

"Grow up, Emily. We had some fun. That's all. A few good fucks." He turned to leave.

She grabbed the fabric of his suit and pulled hard, forcing him to face her. "No!" She stared at him, her eyes going back and forth over his. "That's not all it was. Bull shit! Don't lie to me, Luke. That letter you sent me was one damned lie after another."

Luke swallowed, and she knew everything she said was true.

They stood staring at each other, both of them losing their breath. Emily threw her arms around him, crushing her lips hard against his. It felt so good to feel his hard muscles against her body that she pressed her body tighter against his, as her tongue fought its way inside his mouth.

He stood stiffly against her for a moment before he gave up and slipped his fingers into her hair and pulled her hard against him. His tongue fought hers with a need of desire she had never felt from him before. It only strengthened her need to have him. Both gasped as their breathing sped up.

She put her hands everywhere she could, running them up his chest, slipping her hands inside his jacket then squeezing and rubbing his nipples. She pushed her hands into the hard muscles of his back along his spine, gaining a small moan from Luke. Reaching his ass she squeezed the round globes in her hands and he moaned against her mouth again.

His erection pressed hard against his pants. She could feel it as her hips rotated with their own rhythm against him. She reached down and stroked the rigid length.

"Dammit, Emily," he whispered.

"Fuck me," she begged in his ear. "Fuck me now. Hard."

Instantly his hands cupped her bottom, and he pulled her against him, grinding himself between her legs. He walked forward, pushing her back against the desk, his hands pushing her skirt up around her hips. He reached for her and began stroking her through the tight sheath of her pantyhose, pressing his fingers into her.

She felt herself moisten and the rubbing of his fingers combined with her wetness trapped in the pantyhose sent sparks through her. She rocked herself against his hand. "Oh yes," she said in a breathy whisper. "That feels so good."

He pulled away and with a wicked gleam in his eye, he yanked the pantyhose down her legs, along with her lacy panties. He grabbed her bare ass and lifted her hips high. In one motion he was kneeling on the desk and buried his face between her legs, his tongue an unrelenting tool of pleasure as it licked every inch of flesh it could find.

With her pantyhose still on her calves, she could barely move. The feeling of restraint, of being at the mercy of whatever he wanted, excited Emily more than she'd ever been in her life.

His tongue and lips finally settled on her nub, sucking to create a vacuum and licking the over-sensitive spot until she clenched and cried out as the erotic sensation burst apart, sending electricity flying through her body and white heat throbbing through her.

Her head was on the hard table and through her ragged gasps she heard him unzipping his pants. Lying there in the aftermath of her orgasm she couldn't move. He ripped off one leg of the pantyhose and threw her legs around his hips. He entered her with one swift push that felt like it could burst her in half. Luke gripped her hips hard, pressing his fingers into her flesh so tightly she felt pain. He pounded against her, into her furthest reaches and she cried out with every thrust. At each thundering jab of his rock hard cock, Luke pushed her farther into pleasure. It flooded every cell of her body. Her back arched, every muscle clenched and her heart hammering in her chest as a second orgasm ripped apart her body and mind.

She heard Luke's rapid breaths as he thrust into her again and again, and then his gasp as he released deep inside her, every muscle shaking. After a few more strokes, he stood there, holding himself inside her as his breathing slowed.

He stepped back suddenly and pulled out of her. It left her with a sudden emptiness she didn't want to feel. Wiping his forehead with the back of his hand, he bent down and pulled his pants back on like what they had just done meant nothing.

He gave her a cold look as she lay open and vulnerable before him.

"How was that, Emily-dear?" He smiled at her, the mocking in his eyes more than she could take. "Is that what you believe love feels like?"

She stared at him, her body still shaking with pleasure. A shiver ran down her spine as he stared at her and her body's reaction, not sure what to do with the pleasure and pain mixing together.

"No, *that* was pure, unadulterated selfishness. Yes, I fucking want you. I probably always will. But never for a moment mistake it for love."

"Luke?" she whispered, not sure what to say. His words hurt her more than watching the bullets rip through Gibs' body.

"You're a great fuck, Em." He shrugged before he turned and walked out of the room, shutting the door behind him, leaving her totally alone.

CHAPTER SEVEN

Club Business

During the next three months the tensions with the Rojos skyrocketed. Nothing major happened, but each time the two groups intersected at the Red Bull, or anywhere else, things got tense. Luke did his best to find dirt to get himself out from under the undercover police's noses, but he had nothing to report. At least his ass was still connected to his body and Emily was safe. He hadn't heard from her, not that he expected to. Her safety would have to be enough, though his dreams at night told him he wanted more.

That Friday night, at the Red Bull, Luke wanted to forget thinking about Emily for one night. A group of Westfield Rojos stared him and the Hades' Spawn members down. The quiet evening Luke anticipated at the Red Bull threatened to ignite into a firestorm.

"Those fuckers," said Aces as he, Luke, Dagger, Wolf and a couple of the new brothers hung at the bar. "They're looking for a beat down."

"It's nothing, Aces," said Luke, hoping to defuse the situation.

"They're disrespecting us."

"The Red Bull is neutral ground, man. Rocco doesn't tolerate any violence."

Aces made a noise of disgust. "They'll deserve what they get."

Luke put his hand on Kinney's arm, which drew a warning look from the man. Fortunately, a couple of distractions walked into the bar. Luke didn't who know the women were, but they were just the sort that Kinney found attractive. The girls had their hair teased high and wore too much make-up. Luke waved the women over.

They sauntered toward the table with an over-attempted sexy sway to their hips. A blonde twirled a tendril of hair, giving Luke an appraising look. At Luke's wave Kinney glanced over his shoulder.

"Shit, Spade. How do you get away with that?" growled Kinney.

"My winning personality," grinned Luke. "Can I buy you ladies a drink?"

"Sure, sugar," said the blonde. "What are you drinking?"

"Jack and Coke." Luke expected a large gum bubble to pop out of her mouth. He was almost disappointed when it didn't.

"I'll take the same."

"And what about your friend?"

The girl looked at Luke and then to Kinney, giving him the once over. "What you drinking, hon?" she said.

"Sam Adams," he said, tipping his beer.

"Sounds good."

They were the right amount of distraction. The evening progressed and the Rojos were all but forgotten as the ladies grew friendlier with each drink they downed. Wolf, Dagger and the rest of the crew drifted off to the pool tables.

"How about we find a quieter place for this party," suggested Kinney's girl, whose name turned out to be Jeannie.

"How about we take a walk outside? We can figure out what we want to do," suggested Aces.

"Sure, hon."

"Let's go, then. Come on, Spade."

With a small shake of his head Luke paid for the drinks with a couple of fifties. He trusted John, who would make sure any surplus ran as a credit on his bar tab. The tab was a privilege of being a long-time customer, and Luke was one of the few regulars who had one. This was one reason why Kinney spent most of his time with Luke when they were at the bar. Always looking for a freebie.

Luke followed Kinney and his flavor of the day out to the back of the building. He slipped on his jacket just before he walked out.

"Nice jacket," cooed the blonde, whose name was Austin. She slipped her arm through his and hung close by him.

She didn't smell like Emily. Austin had more of a cheap perfume kind of appeal. Luke shook his head, trying to get Em out of his mind. This was business, not pleasure.

Kinney flipped the switch to the outside lights off, and the concrete and grass disappeared to black. The four of them walked out in the darkness. The July night was hot and sticky. Luke was tempted to take off his jacket again.

"Oh, baby," said Austin, sliding against him, pushing him against the rough boards of the building. Her ample breasts, that couldn't be real, pushed into his chest as her cheap perfume filled his nose. She kissed him hungrily, pressing her form to him, demanding a response.

In the background he heard things getting immediately real for Kinney. The sound of his zipper ripping down his jeans was unmistakable, the slurping noises that soon followed even more so.

"Yeah, sugar. Suck that. You like that don't you, you dirty whore? Take it down, all the way down, slut."

Some people got off on dirty talk but not Luke. He never did, nor could he ever think of women as whores or sluts, even if his companion was doing her best to act like one.

Austin slowly unzipped his jeans and slid her hand inside, rubbing his length. She was obviously trying to mimic the action her friend was already doing. "Feels good, baby, nice and big," she breathed. "Austin would like some of that."

Yeah, he bet she would. Trouble was, since the day he left Emily he hadn't had the inclination. Oh, he had his morning wood, just as he should, but trying to do anything with it proved useless. And now, despite Austin's ardent attentions he didn't even twitch.

He supposed the reason was because of the shitty way he had left Emily, with those awful words and cold exit. Even if he had done it to keep her away from him, to keep her safe, as he descended into the dark underworld of criminal gang activity, he still felt like dirt about it. Thinking about it now wasn't helping his dick.

"Hey, baby," he said to Austin, pulling her hands away. "Save dessert for later. I have an appetizer for you."

His fingers sought her nipple through the thin fabric of her shirt and pinched it hard. She gasped as Luke's other hand reached for the hem of her tight skirt and reached in to find the spot between her legs already dripping wet.

In the dark, Kinney grunted as he worked the throat of the girl on his dick. Luke pulled aside Austin's thin panties and rubbed his thumb around her clit. Her juices slid on his fingers as he swirled around the sensitive spot. She moaned, and impulsively he fisted her hair and pulled back her head, leaving her throat exposed. At the same time he jammed two fingers inside her pussy. Austin gasped, then groaned as he pummeled her with his fingers, his thumb pressed firmly against her clit. She rocked her hips, her breathing hitched, and she gushed all over his hand.

"More!" she gasped as her insides clenched around his fingers.

Luke heard Kinney spit, "Fuck!" Then he moaned, and the girl made gurgling sounds then a spitting noise. "Damn," Jeannie complained.

Austin threw her arms around Luke. "Oh baby. That was a great appetizer. What about the main course?"

Luke pulled out his phone, pretending he had a text. "Sorry, girl. Gotta go." He pulled her arms from around his neck. "Aces, later, man, eh?"

"Sure, Spade," said Kinney, zipping his jeans as Luke walked off into the night. At least he had been able to divert disaster between Kinney and the Rojos, but he didn't feel good about how he had to do it. Not one damn bit.

If this was going to be his life for the next year or longer, he wasn't sure he'd made the right decision.

CHAPTER EIGHT

Life is a Highway

"This looks really good, Luke."

Aces stood next to him the next morning as Luke showed him the clubhouse he built behind his shop.

During the past three months, he had been working hard. He'd bought a Quonset hut kit online for around five thousand dollars, and with the permits, the sewage line, the foundation, the heating system and other building materials, spent an additional fifteen thousand. It was his personal project during the long New England summer as he worked his way into the good graces of Jack Kinney and the now-permanent Tucson crew transplants. He originally thought of putting the clubhouse in the storage garage in back of the shop, but watching a popular television show about outlaw bikers disabused him of that notion. As the tensions with the Rojos ramped up he didn't want his shop the direct target of a Rojos attack. Not saying the clubhouse in the back made it less likely to be hit.

At least it wasn't directly at the back. He built the clubhouse on the other side of the broad blacktop lot behind his shop, the back edge of the Quonset hut hitting the furthest edge of the property. He figured if something did happen, his shop would be out of the line of fire.

He hoped.

"Like we talked about, Aces, the taxes on this building come out of club revenue."

"Don't worry, Luke. We're brothers. You did us right by building the clubhouse. I don't know how Okie got along all these years without one. Besides, you'll come out all right with the rentals of those rooms you built for club members."

"Speaking of which, Pepper's patch comes through tonight, right? He's been on me about one of those rooms since his lease is up and we agreed that only club members could rent a room."

"Well, that's up to the membership, but I haven't heard any objections."

"Good."

"You've become real tight with him since Gibs—"

"Yeah, and since Saks left the club," Luke cut him off. The memory of Gibs' death was still too raw for him. It also reminded him about Emily.

Saks was a bitter pill to swallow too. Saks still worked for him, but with Luke's increasing involvement with what Saks quite rightly saw as a criminal element, Saks barely spoke to him. He simply now came in and did his job. More recently, Saks started taking off a day here and there, and Luke suspected he was looking for another job. Luke couldn't blame him. But it was a tough job market and Luke paid above market wages, so he hoped he wouldn't lose his best mechanic soon. The replacement 'employee' the DEA sent was barely qualified to do simple maintenance and Luke spent more time than he wanted going over the man's work.

"So everything's ready for the inaugural meeting in the new clubhouse?" Aces brought him back to the conversation.

"Yeah."

The liquor permit was the stickiest part of the whole deal, followed by the special permits to allow housing on commercial property. Even private clubs needed a liquor permit in Connecticut. Thanks to the discrete intervention of the DEA, the permit squeaked through just in time. The town zoning regulations couldn't be handled so easily, and Luke had to make special arrangements for that. He hated to skirt the law but small-town politics always won out. There were restrictions too.

He could only make six tiny mini-apartments instead of the ten he wanted due to zoning constraints. He never understood the logic of zoning officials, why six was acceptable but ten was not. But it was better to have something rather than nothing and it gave him extra space to install a couple pool tables. Now, to cover expenses, he had to raise the rent to seven hundred fifty a month instead of the five hundred he had wanted to charge.

What started as a midnight inspiration ended up as a giant summer headache and a royal pain in the ass. Aside from all the challenges, the opening of the clubhouse was nearly accomplished and the smell of the pig roasting to the left of the clubhouse wafted over the parking lot. Pepper came around the side, his face smudged with charcoal.

"What'd you do, Pepper? Start eating that pig?" Luke smiled.

He grinned back. "Man, that porker's falling off the bones already. Good thing you had me put that chicken wire around it."

Luke nodded. Okie taught him that trick on previous club pig roasts. "Well, remember to keep turning it. That center has to be good and cooked through for this evening."

"You got it, boss."

"Don't call me that." He couldn't stand hearing anyone call him boss since Gibs died.

"Sorry, forgot."

"That does smell good." Aces sniffed the air.

"We'll have a good opening. By the time that pig's done it'll literally fall off the bones onto our plates once we clip open that chicken wire." Luke threw his arm around Aces neck briefly in a show of camaraderie he did not feel. "Good drink, good food and good friends."

"Hell yeah! How about a look inside the clubhouse."

Luke shook his head. "Nope. I want it to be a surprise. You'll see it all tonight." He grinned like a proud owner of a shiny new toy, which was a lie. The DEA complained that they couldn't get anything on Kinney because he never discussed any of the club's business in a place where the DEA could listen. Frustrated by the first non-productive weeks of his involvement in their investigation, Luke came up with the idea for the clubhouse. Truth was, a couple of the DEA crew were still inside checking the cameras and bugs they installed inside the club. Luke almost shit a brick when Kinney showed up this morning asking to see the clubhouse.

"Well, later Spade."

"Later."

With relief, Luke watched Kinney get on his bike and pull out of the lot. Pepper walked up to Luke.

"Tell you anything good?"

Luke shook his head. "The little jobs he has me do don't give a clue as to what he's up to."

"Kinney hasn't done shit since the firefight."

"I wouldn't say that. He's padded the membership with the Tucson crew and the new prospects he's recruited. I think he has plans to add some of those as patched members tonight."

"I'm not so sure," said Pepper.

Pepper wasn't sure, but Luke understood what Kinney was doing. Every instinct Luke had said Kinney was getting ready to make a move, but he couldn't do it without the right kind of membership behind him. As the old members of Hades' Spawn moved off in disgust, Kinney brought in men that looked like they'd done time. Pepper's DEA crew confirmed they did.

"He's just gathering his forces is all."

"I hope you're right."

"I am. It's what I would do if I ran a crew like that." He sighed. It was frightening how easy it was for him to think like a criminal. "Okay, get back to that pig. I'm opening the shop."

"Luke."

"What?"

"These six day weeks look like they're killing you. Why don't you let George handle opening and get yourself some breakfast?"

Luke raised an eyebrow. Gone were the days of working half days on Saturday. "What are you, my mother? Being down a man doesn't help my business." Saks, Pepper and Luke had to put in extra hours to cover losing Gibs.

"It's just, I notice you look skin over bones."

"Excuse me?" Luke looked at Pepper in annoyance.

"You look like shit. I can't afford my asset not being at the top of his game."

Luke figured he'd lost some weight because his jeans were loose, but never figured it was noticeable. He took a cigarette out from his pack in his shirt pocket and lit it. He gave up smoking in high school at Emily's urging, but now it didn't seem like there was any reason not to smoke. In fact, there seemed to be many reasons to do so. He drew in the smoke and felt the mild rush of relaxation the tobacco brought him.

"Don't worry about me. Worry about that pig. Or you'll look like shit." *You watch that one and I'll take care of the one working in my shop.*

CHAPTER NINE

Angela's Problem

Emily sat next to her mother waiting for Angela to step out of the dressing room. It was Saturday morning and the bridal store was filled with young brides trying on and displaying dresses, and their wedding parties going through bridesmaid dresses. It seemed busier than what Emily thought a bridal store would be.

A large round stage divided by four walls took the center of the showing room. Curved couches in gray raw silk ringed the stage, spaced apart from each other to give the brides a small aisle to step up on the stage. Behind them were the dressing rooms, two free-standing cubicles per section. Each dressing room had an occupant, and a couple anxious brides-to-be stood next to the cubicles waiting for their turn to try on dresses. When a bride stepped out, she could step up to their section of the stage to show off gowns to their mothers, sisters and bridesmaids.

"We should've come during the week," fretted Emily's mother, "not on Saturday. But we really can't wait, not with the wedding six months away."

Emily almost didn't hear her. She watched the young women in their wedding finery, fighting back her sadness. With the way Luke had talked about getting married she should be one of these women. Not now, not since he pushed her away. She took a quick breath to steady herself. This was all about Angela and she wasn't going to ruin her sister's happiness with her own selfish thoughts.

"Well, one of us works," said Emily dryly. "And I believe that's the bride." She didn't mean to sound miserable. Luckily her mother didn't seem to notice.

One of the waiting brides knocked on the door of the cubicle behind them. Emily turned.

The girl smashing her hand on the door wore flip flops, ripped jeans, and a skinny tank, looking more like a sleaze than a bride. Emily glared at her, somehow the bride reminded her of the last time Emily saw Luke, with those two women hanging off him during Gibs' funeral.

The nascent bride-zilla glared back. "Is she ever going to come out of there? Other people are tired of waitin'!"

Emily's mother tutted, but Emily stood and faced the woman. After what she'd been through, she refused to take shit from anyone ever again. "I'm sure you'd appreciate a little courtesy when it's your turn in there." Emily spoke in a deadly serious voice and the girl shrank back.

But the rude girl was right. Angela was taking longer than she should in the dressing room.

Emily knocked lightly on the door. "Angela, how're you doing in there?"

"I'm fine," said Angela in a small voice. Obviously she was not fine.

Emily tried the door. "Do you need another size?"

That's when Emily heard some snuffles, like Angela was crying. Alarm raced through Emily. "Open up, Ang," she said urgently.

"What's wrong?" Her mother looked up from her chair, clutching her purse.

"Nothing, Mom. I think her zipper's stuck." Emily waved her hand.

"Well, help her."

I'm trying. Emily turned her head so her mother wouldn't see her roll her eyes. How old was she? Nearly thirty and she had to hide her face from her mom? That needed to stop as well.

The door latch clicked and the door opened slightly. Emily slipped in and closed the door. Angela stood in front of the mirror, her eyes lined red. She wore a beautiful all white gown that hugged her skinny curves. Emily's mother picked it out but Angela was reluctant to try it on, but did so at her mother's insistence.

"Hey," said Emily gently, "what's wrong? Is there something wrong with the dress?"

"No. It's beautiful."

"Then what's the problem?"

Angela snuffled again. "I can't wear white."

"What? Of course—"

She stopped talking when she suddenly understood Angela's meaning. Her sister stared at her wide-eyed. "Well, that's no reason not to wear white. It's the twenty-first century, women do it all the time. All the time. That's no reason."

"But this dress is, or will be, too tight."

Emily gave her a quizzical look. "The dress nearly fits. You just get it altered so it's perfect. Probably ninety percent of brides have to get their dress altered. It's not worth cry-stressing over."

"Oh, Emily!" The distress in her sister's whispered voice was evident.

Emily tried to imagine herself in the dress and wondered if she'd be crying because she shouldn't wear white. It seemed silly.

Rattling at the door startled both of them. "Hurry up! It's my turn!"

"Put a sock in it!" snapped Emily. "We'll be out in a minute."

Angela dissolved into a puddle of tears, and Emily took her into her arms.

"I think... I'm pregnant," Angela whispered.

Emily stared at her younger sister. Angela never confided to Emily about how intimate she and Justin were. She just assumed her and Justin were messing around. They were practically married already. Yet here Angela was, shaking like she'd done something wrong.

Of course, in the eyes of the church premarital sex was a sin, even if it was with your fiancé. But in this day and age? Emily figured it was nervousness from the wedding, the possible embarrassment, and what their parents would say.

"Does Justin know?"

"No!" whispered Angela. "I'm not even sure I am. I'm a few days late and just paranoid."

"Come on," said Emily. "Let's get you out of this dress and get out of here. Today's not the day to dress shop. This needs to be special, not nerve wracking."

"But, Mom—"

"She can wait to shop for your wedding dress. She's not the one getting married. How about during the week when it isn't so busy? It's too crowded here to make such an important decision today." She turned her sister around. "Let's ditch Mom at home and you and I are hitting the drug store."

She helped her sister change and left the dress hanging in the change room.

"Mom?" Emily took the reins and guided her sister toward the door. "We're going."

"What?" Amanda Dougherty jumped up and followed the girls. "We really shouldn't wait. Angela, sweetie, we're on a tight schedule as it is."

"It'll be fine, Mom."

"I don't know how she expects to get married in the Fall. Six months is not enough time to plan a wedding."

"Mom," said Emily as she walked her mother to her car and glanced at Angela, looking lost as she headed for the car she and Emily had driven in together to meet their mom at the bridal shop. "A few days won't make any difference. Ang's tired. She's had a busy week, and just needs some rest."

"She's not having second thoughts, is she?"

"Of course not, Mom. You know she usually sleeps at this time of day."

"I suppose."

Emily gave her mother a kiss on the cheek. "I'll be home for dinner later."

"Okay, Emily." Her mother drew in a breath that spoke of her long suffering with her daughters.

Emily resisted the urge to roll her eyes again. "Bye, Mom!" she said cheerily. She turned and walked quickly to Angela's car, where her sister sat bent over, head in her hands. It was unusual to see her sister looking so distraught. She felt bad for Angela. "Start the car, sis. Go find us a drug store." She arched her eyebrows mischievously. "Maybe there's a Vegas wedding in your future."

"Vegas! Oh no, I couldn't." Angela gripped the steering wheel.

"I was only kidding." She glanced at her sister. "Why not, though?"

"I want to get married in the church. I want a beautiful white gown, flowers, flower girls, everything." Angela looked ready to cry again.

"You wanted Prince Charming and fairy castles. Count yourself lucky. You've got the Prince Charming. Others aren't so lucky."

Angela cast a worried glance at Emily. "Oh, Em, I didn't mean—oh, heck. You'll find yours one day."

Emily turned her head and stared out of the window. "There are very few princes out there Angela, but I'm happy for you. Please don't think for a moment I'm not."

"I know you are, Em."

"Hey," said Emily, "don't miss the entrance." She pointed to a Walgreens they were passing.

Angela turned sharply into the parking lot, nearly careening into the landscaping on the right. She jerked the wheel to the left to avoid hitting the bushes.

"Whoa!" cried Emily and then started laughing.

"Sorry," said Angela. "I'm just so worried."

"If you aren't careful, neither one of us will have anything to worry about." She grinned and winked at her sister. "You wait here and I'll go grab a kit. Let me prove to you there's nothing to worry about. I'll be right back."

Angela pulled into a spot in front of the store and Emily hurried in, picking up a shopping basket as she entered. She scanned the aisles quickly and found the feminine products section. She looked at the quantity of pregnancy tests and shook her head, trying to decide which one to get. Finally, she grabbed one that promised early detection. She was about to pull it off the shelf when she caught a movement out of the corner of her eye.

"Hey, Emily."

She knew that voice and whirled around in a panic. "You're supposed to be staying away from me, Evan." She glanced around, ready to run, and then anger took over her fear. She wasn't going to be bullied by this asshole.

"Those orders of protection don't last forever. It expired yesterday, Emily."

"So what? Now you're stalking me again?"

Evan snorted. "I never stalked you. I can't help it if the judge believed that garbage you told him."

Emily pulled her phone out of her purse. "I'm calling the cops right now. How about we see what they think?"

Evan put his hand on hers. "Please don't. I don't want us to fight."

She wrenched her hand away and glared at him. "We're past fighting. Leave me alone, Evan! If you haven't figured it out, I want nothing to do with you."

Evan glanced over her shoulder to the shelves she stood in front of. "Pregnancy test?" He grinned wickedly as he shook his head and tutted. "What's the family going to say?"

"They know you're an ass. Now leave me alone!" She pivoted and grabbed a pink box as she hurried away from her ex. She shook, but not from fear. It was rage. She was so angry. Why the hell would he confront her in the store? She definitely would have to get the order extended. Whatever it took. She hadn't seen him in months and figured he'd finally moved on.

At the cash register her hands shook when she took out her debit card. She barely paid attention to the price ringing up. It seemed higher than normal but she didn't care. She just wanted the cashier to tell her the total and let her pay and get out of there.

"You sure you need a combo pack, Ma'am?"

"Pardon?" Emily stared at the girl, trying to figure out what she meant.

"Most people only get one pack. Do you want to change it?"

The cashier held up the box and Emily realized it had three pregnancy tests in it instead of one. Looking over her shoulder, she saw Evan heading toward the same check-out line she was in. "It's fine. They're not for me."

"Sure, Ma'am," the cashier said with a knowing look that meant she clearly didn't believe her.

Wanting to get away as quickly as possible, Emily didn't argue. She swiped the debit card, grabbed the bag and jogged back to Angela's car. "Let's go!" she said, slamming the door shut quickly.

"What's wrong?" Angela pulled the car into reverse. She still looked anxious but at least she hadn't been crying.

"Evan!" Emily hissed. "He came up to me in the store."

"What a jerk! Hold on. I'll get us out of here." Angela reversed then shoved the car into drive before peeling out of the drug store parking lot like her tires were on fire.

"Was he following you?" Angela asked as she glanced out the rear view mirror.

"I don't know. I don't think he'd wait for us at a bridal store. I haven't seen him in months. I thought he'd moved on with his life."

Angela snorted. "The guy doesn't have a life."

"I'll have to renew the restraining order. Or whatever it is you have to do to get it extended. Apparently it expired yesterday."

"I'll ask Justin. He'll know."

They drove in silence the rest of the way to Angela's house. Evan didn't follow and Emily let herself relax. Maybe it had just been a coincidence. A scary, freak coincidence.

They headed inside and Emily sent her sister straight to the bathroom with a stick.

"I don't know if I can do this," Angela said through the bathroom door. "What am I supposed to do? You have the box."

"It couldn't be easier. Just pee on the end of the stick."

Angela became quiet, and a minute later Emily heard the toilet flush.

"How long?" called Angela through the door a few minutes later.

"The box says five minutes," Emily replied.

"This is the longest five minutes of my life. Nothing's happening."

"Well, that's a good sign."

"What if there's something wrong with the test?" Angela opened the door and pointed to the stick on the sink. "I don't think I did it right."

"We have two others if we need them." Emily came in carrying the kit.

"Emily, I really think something is wrong with the test. Nothing's showing in the display window."

"Give it another minute, Ang."

Angela picked up the white stick and held it out to Emily. "Look, there's only one faint line. It doesn't even look like a line. Maybe it's too early to test. Maybe one line means yes." She grabbed the box from Emily and checked the side.

"Pregnant would be two lines. So you aren't if there's only one."

Angela shook her head. "I don't believe it. I think the sticks expired or something. Maybe it read wrong somehow."

"Here, gimme one. I'll show you. I'll do one myself. You'll see the exact same result." She unwrapped the test stick.

"Not while I'm in here! Eww!" Angela rushed out of the bathroom and closed the door behind her.

Emily laughed. "Like you've never seen me pee!"

"Not since I was like five!"

Laughing, she peed on the end of the stick for five seconds like the test said and waited. One line came up, a little darker than Angela's but similar. She opened the door and showed Angela. "See, there is nothing wrong with the test."

Angela gingerly took the end of the stick that was clean. She looked at it and then at her sister. "Are you sure? Because there are two lines here."

"No, there isn't."

"Look!"

Emily took the stick back from her sister and stared it at. She couldn't believe that second line would come out in the space of handing it to Angela.

Angela started giggling. "Now are the sticks off?"

"They must be." She couldn't take her eyes off the stick, except to check her watch. It had been less than two minutes and two lines?

Angela pushed her out of the bathroom. "Let me try the third stick."

Emily stood outside the door staring at the stick. She'd always been irregular and never paid much attention, but how long ago had she seen Luke? Three months? She would have noticed something, right? The sticks had to be off.

Angela came out with the stick. "Same line on mine. Like the other one."

"Oh shit." Emily covered her mouth.

"You didn't know?" Angela looked partially relieved it wasn't her. "Do you think you are? Have you noticed any symptoms?"

"I don't know. Sore boobs I guess. I just figured it's because I've been sleeping on my back or that my period was coming. Not that bad though."

"What about puking?" Angela took the stick from Emily and shoved it in the box.

"Maybe. I don't know. Maybe a little nauseous in the mornings but nothing like mom described. I just figured it was because I was upset about everything's that happened."

"Do we need another kit?"

Emily shook her head and sighed. "I'm pretty sure I'm pregnant. How I didn't notice..." She sighed again, this time it came out shaky.

"Is it Luke's baby?"

"Who else?"

"Well, you and Evan..." Angela let the words hang in the air.

"No!" spit Emily. "Evan and I never, ever went all the way. We argued about that. I guess I knew deep inside he wasn't for me."

"What're you going to do?"

"Do? I have no idea." She touched her belly. Could she really be carrying Luke's baby? It couldn't be true.

"You have to tell him."

"No!"

"He needs to know."

Emily wanted to cry. She trudged to Angela's living room and dropped down in the first seat. "Luke made it quite clear he wanted nothing to do with me."

"But—"

"No buts, Ang. Don't tell Mom and Dad. Please?" She knew she sounded silly but she didn't want anyone to know. She needed to absorb the information on her own.

"You can't do this on your own!" Angela pressed her lips tight. "That Luke Wade! He left you a mess in high school and now he's gone and done it again. I'd like to give him a piece of my mind!"

Emily tried not to smile, despite the seriousness of the situation. Her sister's idea of a piece of her mind would be equivalent to having a gummy bear beat up a giant. "Don't you even think about seeing Luke Wade!" Emily sighed. "I'll take care of this myself."

"How?"

"I don't know."

"You can't do this on your own. Maybe adoption? You wouldn't..." Angela's eyes grew big at the thought of what she couldn't say.

"No!" Emily shook her head. "No, Ang. If I'm big enough to get myself into this situation, I'm adult enough to deal with the consequences."

"What would you do? Live with Mom and Dad? You couldn't drive yourself to the hospital if you were in labor. What about—"

"Geez, Angela! I need time to think. I can't answer any of that now." She sank against the back of the chair. Pregnant? How was she going to handle this? She had no job, no health insurance, and now, being pregnant, no one would want to hire her. And everything else? Baby furniture, clothes, diapers. Raising a kid was expensive! She buried her head in her hands. "I sure fucked up this time."

CHAPTER TEN

Neutral Ground

Luke didn't dislike George, but he got impatient with incompetence. The DEA sent George undercover because the man claimed he knew how to repair bikes. He must have meant bicycles. George had a shade tree mechanic's understanding of motorcycle engines and could barely replace brake pads. Luke did his best to give him simple jobs, but the truth of it was that Luke's reputation was built on his ability to repair high-performance bikes. Harley engines mandated a master's level of knowledge. Gibs had known, Saks had the skills, and Pepper was learning it. But George didn't, and would never be good. It was a problem. A big one.

Luke grabbed his iPad off his desk.

"Hey, George." Luke tried to sound positive. "What're you doing there?"

"Well, the complaint is stalling and rough idle. I thought I'd change the spark plugs and see what happens."

Luke shook his head. "Most likely it's the electronic fuel injection sensor."

"How do you know?"

"Because you can trust an electronic component to fail before a piece of hardware does. Those things are cranky even in Harleys. Leave it for Saks."

"But," George said as Luke gave him a warning look. He wasn't going to listen to George's argument about being in first today.

"Look." Luke clenched his jaw before continuing, "I've no doubt you're damn good at what you do, but this is my business and I can't afford to fuck up anyone's bike. Play the part of the eager intern all you want, but you aren't handling the big stuff."

"I can do it."

Luke sighed, his patience wearing thin. "No, you can't. There are guys who go to Harley College to learn how to do this work." *Not pomp-ass little police shits trying to ruin my life and my shop!*

"Harley College?"

"They certify as Harley mechanics through certain schools."

"Did you go to one of these schools?"

He'd had enough. "Don't you have a fuckin' dossier on me to check that shit?" he snapped. "Of course I did. Did it through the G. I. Bill."

"I still can't believe you served, man."

"Yeah, neither does the Navy." He shoved his iPad toward George. "Go do the inventory."

"Again?"

"Yeah, and each time I tell you. You missed five fuel injectors on the last one. Nearly gave me a heart attack."

George opened his mouth to argue, which was always a mistake, but shut it when the distinctive roar of several Harley engines rattled the open garage doors.

Luke stepped to the entrance and nearly shit his pants. Four Rojos sat on various models and model years of Harleys, ranging from the eighties to the first decade of the millennium. The Rojos sat on their bikes poised in front of the entrance, letting their engines idle. The ominous rumbling of the bikes drew George to the entrance as well.

"You the owner?" called out the foremost rider to Luke above the sound of the engines. The man was dark skinned and his face round. His unruly dark long hair held back by the Rojos trademark red bandana. He wore the standard Rojos uniform, denim cut, blue jeans and a white wife beater. His shoulders were hunched a bit, folding in the cut toward his chest so Luke couldn't see the exact patches, but there were a number of wings, which did not testify to the man's good character.

"Yes."

"I hear you fix bikes."

"You could say that," Luke said tersely. He stared down the man, wondering what the hell the Rojos were doing at his shop.

"I've got an oil leak no one can find. I hear you're the best."

"Yeah? You sure you want me to fix it?" Luke crossed his arms, careful not to sound angry. "I'm sure you've heard I'm not in good standing with your club."

"Yeah, I got that *pendejo*. But when it comes to my ride I don't care what color yellow you are. If you can fix it, I'll pay. So, let's just say for today, your shop is neutral territory."

Luke looked away then turned back and slowly nodded. "Okay, man. But don't fuck with me. My friends wouldn't like that."

"Do I have to wave a fucking white flag? My baby's ailing here and I can't afford to lose her."

Luke walked over to the bike. He whistled as he looked over the bike. "What is it? A 2007 Sportster?" His interest in the bike outweighed the trouble of the rival club.

"Yeah, it was my old man's."

"You mean your old lady's," joked one of the other guys on a bike.

"*Silencio*," hissed the Rojos.

Luke knelt beside the bike to examine it while the Rojos had it idling. "I've a 2009 Sportster," Luke explained, "one of the pearl orange ones. It's a bike made for speed like yours." He straightened and tapped the handlebar. "But your baby's eight years old and looks like it can use some deep maintenance, a little more than changing the oil and brakes. Hop off and I'll take it into the bay."

"No fuckin' way. No one rides my bike but me."

"And your mechanic. Insurance says either me or one of my employees takes it into the bay. Or you'll have to take it somewhere else."

The guy shook his head. "No, man. They call me Pez."

"Pez, eh?"

"Yah, cuz the *hombre* can't keep his mouth shut."

"Who's talking, eh, *cabron?*"

Reluctantly, the man got off his bike. Luke stuck out his hand. "My street name's Spade."

"Spade, eh? For a white guy like you?"

"*Tal vez no tan blanco,*" said Luke.

"*Como*?"

"My mom was French, from Hispaniola, though my dad was Mexican."

"So how you end up here, *ese*?"

"Bad luck," said Luke with a smile.

The Rojos laughed. "I can see that." Pez slapped him on the back. "I like you, man."

Luke settled into the saddle of the bike. "I'll take her in then. You can go in the office and wait there. Or there's a coffee shop over in the next lot."

"No fuckin' coffee. I want to watch the work."

"Then open the door to the shop, just don't step in." He shrugged. "Insurance, again."

"*No necesita esperar para mí. Te llamare,*" said Pez to his companions.

With some grumbling the Rojos rode off.

Luke might not like the Rojos in general, but this guy Pez seemed all right. Luke watched him walk toward the office and caught the territory name off the man's bottom rocker on his cut.

Bridgeport.

Well, fuck, Luke thought. Bridgeport to Westfield was a forty mile trip one way. Bridgeport was once a large manufacturing center, but now it was riddled with poverty and decay. To the people of nice, safe, middle-class Westfield it was another county. It was highly unlikely the man showed up of his own volition. The message was clear. Someone sent him here.

Why?

With Pez watching him through the open door, Luke pulled the Sportster in the bay closest to the entrance and put it on the lift. He pulled it up slightly so he could get a good look all around and didn't see where the leak could be. Pez was right. It was a hidden leak.

"George, go over to the barber shop next to the coffee shop and ask if I can borrow a can of talcum powder."

"Talcum powder?"

"Just do it, George."

"Sure, Luke."

While Luke waited for George, he cleaned out the gunk at the bottom of the engine with spray engine cleaner, wiping it away with a clean soft cloth. When George returned, Luke put a small amount of powder in his hand and blew a fine mist of it over the bottom of the engine. Lowering the bike he started the engine and let it idle.

Pez looked at him with disbelief and called out, "You gonna fix my bike with barber powder? What? Want to give it a sexy smell?"

"Just give it some time." The minutes ticked tensely by as the engine idled and no oil appeared. The engine was almost getting too hot to idle. Then a small dark spot appeared on the white talcum. Luke almost sighed in relief and turned off the engine. "Here it is. It isn't engine oil at all. It's gear oil from your tranny that's slipping out from the clutch cable. No wonder your mechanic couldn't find it."

"No, *pendejo. My* mechanic did. So what'll it cost to fix it?"

"It's mostly labor. We have a two-hour minimum." Luke did the math. "Two hundred fifty bucks."

"I see." Pez grimaced.

Luke realized the man couldn't afford it. He glanced at the shop clock. Damn, Saks was late, again. He would have to do this repair himself. That wasn't a problem, but he worried what would happen if one of his regular customers came in and saw the outlaw biker in his office.

What the fuck you worried about, Wade? he said to himself. *Isn't that what the Spawn are becoming?* It was true. He knew it. This man was sent here to find out how much. Everything Luke said and did was being evaluated. This biker must be highly respected by state leadership if he was sent to do this reconnaissance.

Luke wiped his hands with a clean towel. "I'll tell you what. This'll take me an hour if I have no distractions. I'll give you a one-time only friends and family discount if you tell people what a good job I did. Say a hundred twenty-five."

"All I have to do is say nice things about you?" Pez arched an eyebrow.

"Not me. You can call me a *pendejo* if you want. Just say that Luke Wade is a *pendejo*, but he's a wizard at fixing bikes."

The man relaxed, taking Luke's meaning. Luke didn't expect to be exonerated from the Rojos' thinking of him.

Pez chuckled. "I think I can handle that, *pendejo*."

"Good." Luke turned back to the bike and went to work right away. He worked steady to take off the tranny box, clean it out, replace the seals and fill it back with gear oil. The work was nearly finished when Pepper walked into the bay from the back garage door and stopped short when he saw the Rojos watching his boss work.

"Pez, Pepper. Pepper, Pez," said Luke, waving an Allen wrench he was using to put the tranny box back together. He then fixed it back onto the bike with sure, swift turns of his wrench. "Okay, that does it. All it needs is a test run."

"Naw," said Pez. "I've got to run. Thanks, man. I'll run by the cash to you next Friday."

Pepper stared at Pez, knowing that Luke only delivered a bike when payment was made.

"Okay," said Luke, which caused Pepper's eyes to nearly bug out. "But Friday it is, or I'll put a curse on it and you'll find out I'm not a wizard but a *voudin*. Because you know what they practice on Hispaniola."

"Don't worry, *ese*. You'll have your cash."

Luke rolled the bike out to the parking lot and handed it over to Pez, who started it and raced off.

"What the fuck was that all about?" Pepper came up behind him.

"I don't know, but I think I just got Central Valley Bike Repair declared neutral ground." He slapped Pepper on the shoulder. "Not bad for a morning's work, eh?"

"Fuck, no," said Pepper in awe.

"Good. Now get on that bagger. And put George on the pig. The man's nearly useless with the bikes anyway." Luke looked at the shop's clock again and sighed. "It looks like Saks won't be in today."

CHAPTER ELEVEN

Amanda Dougherty's Secret

After she left Angela's, Emily turned to the one person she could talk to. She sat in Mrs. Diggerty's kitchen eating a chocolate chip cookie the woman had just made. Reger rubbed up against her legs now, enjoying privileges in both apartments. In the past three months he ran back and forth between them begging for food and getting fat while he did so. Once Emily and Mrs. Diggerty compared notes they agreed to each give Reger half a small can each day, Emily in the morning and Mrs. Diggerty at night.

Emily felt more confused than earlier. No matter how she turned the thoughts over in her head she couldn't come up with an answer. She knew she had to tell her parents, but wanted to talk to someone about everything before she did. It was easy for her to talk to her landlady because the dear woman never judged her, unlike her parents.

"I don't know what I'm going to do," she said. "I don't know if I can raise it alone."

Mrs. Diggerty set a teacup for Emily, and herself. She sat down and poured the tea from a pot sitting on the table.

"Why couldn't you adopt out your child?" Mrs. Diggerty said as she sat in the chair opposite Emily. "There are thousands of parents who desperately want a child."

"I can't bear the thought of giving up this child, but on the other hand, I don't know." She stared at the steam lifting off her tea. "It's not that he or she wouldn't have a good home. I just feel a connection to this baby. He's..." Emily let the words trail as tears welled in her eyes.

"Because he's part of someone you love," said Mrs. Diggerty gently.

"Yes," Emily whispered.

"I can't imagine what you're going through. But I think there is one thing for sure. You shouldn't make a decision until you talk to the father."

Emily looked up at the ceiling and sucked in a breath. "I already know what he'll say. He made it clear he didn't want to have anything to do with me."

"You know, sweetheart. I can't believe that. I remember that day he sat on the porch waiting for you. I'd never seen a young man look so anxious."

"You saw him?"

"When I came in from an errand, yes. I asked who he was, and he told me. He even asked if I thought you'd like the flowers he brought."

"He did?" Emily fingered the necklace he gave her that day. She'd never taken it off.

"Yes. And I tell you, love was shining in his eyes when he spoke your name. You couldn't miss it."

"Well, he doesn't love me now," she said with bitterness in her voice. "Things change."

"Perhaps. Perhaps not. But it's his child too. He may want to help you for the baby's sake. Hell, you can make him help you, if you take him to court."

Emily's head shot up at the sounds of her little old landlady swearing. If she wasn't so stressed, she'd have laughed. "I could never make someone do something if they didn't want to. Plus, I've had enough of courts."

"That's your pride talking," Mrs. Diggerty said.

"Maybe it is," admitted Emily. "But you don't know what he was like the last time I saw him. He was so... cold." She lowered her head as the shame she felt when he left her that day in the funeral home office washed over her again.

"I don't pretend to understand men, Emily. But right is right. You have to give him a chance."

"Well, I have other people I should tell first. I need time to think."

"Take all the time you need."

When Emily got her bail money back from the court she bought a car. She'd searched for a month on Internet ad sites and after looking at a few clunkers, she found the perfect one for her. It was a fifteen-year-old black Sebring, but the original owner had taken good care of it. The paint was flawless and the metal rims were as shiny as the day it rolled out of the factory. She could hardly believe her luck when her mechanic told her he'd never seen an older car in such good shape. She bought it immediately and considered herself lucky she didn't have to make a car payment, especially since she didn't have a job.

Her parents' home was set on the corner of two streets. The driveway sat on the left-hand side of the house, with hedges lining either side of it. She entered through the side door of the house, to the kitchen. She heard voices and her stomach tightened again. It sounded like both her parents were home.

With a sigh she walked through the bright and perpetually clean kitchen into the dining room. She followed the voices to the living room and stopped short.

"What're you doing here?" She thought she was going to faint.

Evan looked up at her, his expression all innocence. Why the hell would her parents let him in?

"I was just telling your mom here that I'd do the right thing."

"What?" Emily yelled. She looked toward her mother, whose face was blanched white.

"You're pregnant!" she said, her voice a hoarse whisper. "How could you? This is not how you were raised."

"Evan has no business being here! Or telling you I'm pregnant!" This was not bloody happening. This had to be some kind of a nightmare.

"But Emily, if he's the father—"

"He's NOT the father!" Emily clenched her fists. "Get the hell out of here, Evan Waters!"

Evan stood, crossing his arms over his chest, a triumphant look on his face. "You can't keep ignoring me, Emily. Especially now."

"OUT!" Emily was so upset she was shaking. She pointed to the door with her finger.

"I'll demand a paternity test."

"Demand all you want. You're delusional, especially if you think this child has anything to do with you!"

Evan sighed dramatically. He smiled kindly at her mom. "I'm sorry she's so upset. It must be the hormones." He moved to the front door. "I'll talk to you soon, Mrs. D."

"You WILL not!" yelled Emily.

"We'll talk to you when you're not so upset." Evan walked quickly to the door and let himself out.

Emily was breathing hard, almost hyperventilating. "I can't believe him! I can't believe you! Why would you let him in?"

"Emily, are you going to tell me what is going on?"

She stomped over to her mother. "Evan got it half right, but only because he saw me buying a pregnancy test. Yeah, I'm pregnant. But hell no! Not by Evan Waters!" She couldn't believe her mother had freakin' let him into the house. How messed up was this family?

"Who then?" Her mother's face was drawn tight. "Not that Wade boy."

"Man, mother! Luke's a man." She'd never been this angry before. She couldn't believe life could be this ridiculous. "And he's the father."

"How can you be sure?" said her mother, biting her pinky.

"Because I'm not the fuck up you think I am," she shouted. "I slept with Luke. Period. End of story."

"But you aren't seeing him anymore."

"You're just filled with stunning insights, aren't you?"

"Emily! Don't talk to me like that. And stop swearing."

"Then don't talk to me like I'm an idiot, mother. I'm not. I may have made a mistake—"

"It's a very big mistake."

"Again, I'm not stupid. I realize the gravity of the situation. I would hope that my *mother* would, at least, be understanding. I don't think that's too much to ask."

"But you've sinned, Emily. You broke one of the Ten Commandments."

Really? "Sins can be forgiven, mother. Insensitivity cannot."

"Insensitive? You think I'm insensitive?" Her mother's voice went up an octave.

"I'm pregnant! I'm terrified. And all you can think about is my sin?" Her mother's mouth dropped open but Emily continued, "Why did you want to keep me away from Luke? Why were you so against him?"

"I was only trying to protect you! So you wouldn't go through what I did."

"What?" said Emily, walking toward her mother. "What did you go through?"

Her mother rose. "Like you. Pregnant. The boy didn't want to have anything to do with me."

Emily stared at her mom, her brows pressed together. Her heart suddenly sped and the room spun. She rested a hand on the back of a chair. "Wait, are you telling me, Dad isn't my dad?"

"Don't you start that Emily Rose Dougherty! In all the ways that count, he's your father. He's loved you like his own from the day you were born."

Could today get any more shocking? Except, in a weird way, it made sense. But still!!! "Who's my father?" When her mother didn't answer, Emily raised her voice. "Who's my father?!"

"It doesn't matter. He's in prison. He won't be out for a long time."

"What? Prison?" Who's the friggin' sinner now? She wanted to snap at her mom, but bit her lip from saying it out loud when she noticed how her mother was suddenly acting.

Her mother seemed lost in her own thoughts as she began to pace. "No. I won't tell you. I promised your father I wouldn't tell you. You won't get any more out of me!"

Emily shook her head, unsure of what to do as she watched her mother seemingly change into someone she didn't know.

"Didn't you ever wonder why you never saw my parents? Your grandparents?" She spun around and paced again, oblivious to the tears running down her face. She threw her hand toward the wall where framed photos hung. "Not even a picture!"

"You said they died before we were born."

Amanda Dougherty shook her head and laughed. "They disowned me, Emily! Kicked me out of the house." She snapped her fingers. "Just like that! You want to talk about insensitive?"

"Mom," Emily said quietly. "I never knew. I'm sorry."

Amanda snorted. "If it wasn't for your father, I don't know what I would've done."

"Oh, mom. That's the saddest thing I ever heard."

Her mother sniffed and wiped at her eyes. "I needed their help, and they turned their back on me."

"I'm so sorry." Emily's own tears began blurring her mother's face.

"It's not your fault, Emily." She stopped pacing and took a moment to gather herself. "It was mine. I think I took it out on you anyway, a little, by being so strict with you. I thought that if I made sure you were good, nothing would happen to you."

"Mom, it doesn't work like that."

"I'm not so sure." She looked ready to cry again. "We are all punished for our sins."

"I'm not punishment." Could her mother really believe that? She didn't think so, but after today... she wasn't sure. "I see this baby—my baby—as a blessing. The timing is just really off."

"Maybe." Her mother sighed but didn't sound very convinced. She sat down and Emily came over and sat beside her. She gave Emily a strained smile. "Just so you know, Emily. I've always loved you and I won't do to you what my parents did to me."

Emily put her arms around her and gave her a hug. "I'm glad to hear that. I love you too."

Her mother pulled back and straightened her skirt. Strain was clearly written across her face. "Now, I just have to figure out how to tell your father."

"I'll tell him."

"No, I don't think that's a good idea. I think I should."

"Mom, I'm not sixteen years old anymore. I'm almost thirty."

"You're still our little girl."

"She what?"

Sam Dougherty exploded so loud Emily heard him shouting from the first floor to the second. She gulped. Even though her mother pleaded with her to wait in her old bedroom, Emily didn't feel it was right to leave her mother to face her father alone. She crept down the stairs, the bearing wall that ran to the roof where the stairs climbed the only defense against her father's wrath.

"Now, Sam. Calm down."

"Calm down! How dare she? After all we've done for her."

"I know you are upset—"

"Upset doesn't begin to cover it! Where is she?"

"In her room, but Sam—"

"Don't 'but Sam' me, Amanda." He spun and shouted out, "Emily Rose Dougherty, get your butt down here!"

Emily rounded the wall to the living room. "You don't have to yell, Dad."

She'd never seen Sam Dougherty so angry. At that moment, all the connection she felt for him crumbled. He wasn't her father. She didn't share a bit of his DNA. For most of her life all she remembered was Sam Dougherty being upset, or disagreeable, or demanding. As a young girl he made her tremble. When she was older, all he did was make her angry. The thought scared her.

"What do you have to say for yourself?"

"Say? What would you have me say, *dear daddy?*"

Her mother winced at Emily's tone.

"Explain yourself!"

"I think the words 'I'm pregnant' are pretty self-explanatory."

"Don't be sarcastic with me!"

Emily sighed. "I know you're disappointed, but being angry won't change it. Things are as they are. I wanted to tell you before anyone else did. Mom convinced me to let her tell you. That mistake is mine." She grabbed her purse and walked toward the back door.

"Just where do you think you are going?"

"I'm doing what I should've done a long time ago. I'm growing up. I'll let you know how it works out."

CHAPTER TWELVE

A New Complication

Saks didn't show nor did he call, which pissed Luke off, but what was he going to do? He couldn't drag the man to work by his heels. Saks wouldn't answer his phone either. Luke's calls went straight to voicemail. He supposed the six day workweeks, and the lack of the weekly road trips that used to be the highlight of their week, had gotten to Saks. He just wanted a day off. Luke didn't blame him, but he did expect the courtesy of a phone call.

The day wound through, and between him and Pepper they managed to get a lot of the work done. Luke supposed he'd have to come in tomorrow to catch up on the week's work. The thought didn't please him at all.

He stood from the bike he was working on when he heard the doorbell ring with the opening of the office door. Luke expected it would be a customer picking up his bike. He was wrong.

"Hey, Luke," said Wanda.

"Hey, what's going on?"

"I hate to bother him at work, but can I talk to Tony?"

"He's not here."

"He left? Already?"

"He never showed, Wanda. I figured he just wanted a day off."

"Oh," she said, biting her lip. "We were supposed to go out last night, but he never showed."

A sense of alarm shot through Luke. Maybe Saks would blow him off, but he wouldn't do that to a date, especially with a girl he liked as much as Wanda. "I'm sure there's a good reason. Tell you what. When I see him I'll tell him you asked about him."

"Sure, Luke."

"And if you want, stop by in a bit and have some barbecue with us."

Wanda shook her head. "I don't think so, but thanks for asking me."

"Okay. I'll make sure he gets a hold of you when I see him." Luke waved goodbye with a sour feeling in his stomach. If it had been the old group, Wanda would have gladly joined them, but a nice gal like Wanda didn't want anything to do with the current group of club members. Luke couldn't blame her. He was actually glad she was staying away.

Except now he was worried about Saks. "Hey, Pepper?"

Pepper walked into the office wiping grease from his hands with a shop rag. "What's up?"

"Saks didn't show for his date with Wanda last night."

"He didn't show for work today." A single eyebrow rose.

"I'm going to his apartment to check things out."

"What's his phone number?"

"Why?"

"I can have my guys get a location where the phone is."

"I thought you needed a court order for something like that."

"A lot of people think a lot of things. Most of it isn't true."

Luke gave him Saks' phone number. "I'll be back within the hour."

"You better be. This cookout is a big deal now and my people are looking forward to seeing how things turn out."

"I know. You've got my number?"

"Yeah, why?"

"Just in case."

Luke took his 2014 Iron 883 from the storage garage and grimly swung out onto the road, the Sportster's engine rumbling between his legs. A sick feeling gripped his stomach as he rode toward Saks' apartment. Inside, he knew he wouldn't find Saks there and his worry levels soared. Things didn't get any better when he reached the apartment building. In the marked parking slot for Saks' apartment sat his bike, covered in a bike tarp.

"Fuck!" mumbled Luke. There was no way Saks went anywhere without his bike unless it was the dead of winter. For that time of year, Saks had a "beater" car, a sad collection of rust, bondo and an engine that rumbled more than his motorcycle. But that cage was parked in the back of Luke's lot during the summer so Saks wasn't in it either.

Luke took the stairs to his employee's apartment and knocked on the door. He tried to peer into the window beside the door but the apartment was dark.

"Hey, what's up?"

Luke swung in the direction of the unfamiliar voice. A man in his forties wearing overalls stood holding a paint can and some brushes.

"I'm looking for Saks, I mean, Tony. I'm his boss and he didn't show for work today. It's not like him."

"Yeah, Tony usually pays his rent on this day of the month, every month like clockwork. He didn't show either."

"His bike's in his parking slot. His girlfriend came by and said he didn't show for their date last night."

"He's got that old car of his."

"It's parked behind my shop for the summer."

The older man scratched his head. "I'm the super. I suppose it wouldn't hurt anything if I poked my head in." His hands went into one of the pockets of his overalls and pulled out a keychain thick with different keys. Luke stepped aside and the super opened the door.

"Hey! Tony? It's me, Jack. Tony?"

"Do you see anything?"

"His place looks a little messy."

"Messy? That's not like him. Let me see."

"I shouldn't."

"Look, all of this doesn't sound like Tony."

"All right. But don't go inside."

Luke poked his head inside the door. As he suspected, things were more than a little messy. Papers and dishes were strewn on the floor and furniture pushed out of place. Luke's jaw set as he gazed at the scene. There had been a scuffle.

"Don't you have some plumbing you need to check in here?"

"No," the man said slowly.

Luke pulled out a fifty from his wallet. "I'd appreciate it if you check the plumbing. I'll wait out here."

"Put your money away. I like Tony just fine." The super put down his paint can and shoved open the door. "Mr. Parks! It's me, Jack. I'm just going to check your faucets."

There was no answer, and the man walked in. It didn't take him long to return, his face ashen white.

"He's not there. There's some blood on the wall in the kitchen."

"How much blood?"

"Enough that it wasn't an accident. I'm calling the police."

"You do that. I'll go check on some other things."

There was only one place that Luke could think to get some answers. He hopped on his bike and headed toward the Red Bull.

He jumped off on his bike, counting the bikes at the bar and parked his by the front. He headed inside.

A band was playing at full volume in the crowded bar. Luke made his way to the bar and waited until John turned toward him.

"Hi, Luke," said John, his eyebrows raised in surprise. "I thought tonight is your big shindig. In fact, a woman was in here a little earlier looking for you. I told her you'd be there. What you having?"

"A draft." John's comment about a woman looking for him was a usual thing and something he didn't pay attention to anymore. Since he'd been hanging around with Kinney he picked up as many girls as Kinney did. "The clubhouse opening is tonight. I was hoping to see Saks there."

"I'm sure he won't miss it."

"Well, that's the thing. He didn't show up for work today, and he missed a date with one of his favorite girls last night, so now I don't know what to think."

John's face drew into a frown, but before he could say anything a patron called his name. "I'll be right back," the bartender said.

While Luke waited he felt a hand on his shoulder. His head snapped around to find Pez at the other end of the hand.

"What you doing here, *pendejo*? I thought you were having a big party tonight?"

"What do you know about that?"

"*Everyone* knows, *blanco*." Pez dropped his arm from Luke's shoulder.

Luke gauged the look on the man's face and immediately alarm shot through his body. "Is there going to be trouble?" he asked.

Pez shrugged. "Depends on what your *hombre*, Aces, does."

"What? What's going on, Pez?"

"That's some *cabron* you have there running things, blanco. He's got the Hombres and the Rojos snapping at each other. We delivered a message to him to back off, but I don't think he's taking it."

"Message? What message?"

Pez took out his cell phone and held it to Luke's face. With horror, Luke saw Saks, his forehead streaked in crusted blood, tied to a chair.

Luke grabbed Pez by his cut.

"Where is he? He's got nothing to do with Ace's shit."

Around them people stopped talking and stared. A sharp whistle pierced the air. Both Luke and Pez turned their heads to the sound.

"Take it outside, boys," said John.

"John, man. You don't understand." Luke ripped the cell phone from Pez's hand and slapped it on the bar.

John stared at the picture and then his face turned red. "Outside! Both of you! Sally, yo," he called to the waitress. "Watch the bar."

John marched both of the men out the back door. Pez retrieved his phone on the way. "What the fuck's going on?"

"Ask the *pendejo* here," shot Pez.

"I am asking you, because sure as shit, Luke had nothing to do with this."

Pez held up his hands.

"Don't shoot the messenger. We all, I mean, all of us in the Rojos got this picture. Hombres leadership don't like outsiders messing in our shit."

John poked his finger into Pez's chest. "You go back to your leadership and tell them that they've taken on more shit than they can handle. Anthony here is family. Or more like, *familia.* Get that, *cabron.* Tony better be back here at the Red Bull in two hours or every single one of you are going to wish your papas never came to Connecticut."

Pez gave John a cheeky grin. "Believe it or not, I'm on your side, *blanco*. I hate this crap. It's bad for business. I'll deliver your message. I'll just take this *pendejo* with me. He'll bring your Anthony back, or neither one of them will return. I can't say either way."

"Luke?"

"Yeah, I'm good with that." He didn't have a choice.

"Then get out of here, *cabron*. The clock's ticking."

Pez moved toward the parking lot, but John grabbed Luke's arm. "Here," he said, drawing a handgun from behind his vest in the back. "Can you shoot?"

"Yeah, but John—"

"Just take it. Get my cousin out of there or my grandmother will shoot me."

Luke gave John a steely gaze, though he was blown away with what he just learned. "I'll do my best."

"I'd go myself, but I don't have permission, and that would take a while to get everyone together. You understand?"

"I didn't know you were connected." Wiseguys were woven into the warp and woof of Connecticut, but Luke never imagined Rocco and his brother were part of it.

"There are a lot of things you don't know about me, Spade. Just know this. We won't be fucked with."

"Yeah, I get that." It was all he could say. The Rojos and the Hombres stepped into a pile of shit of unimaginable proportions. Saks' kidnapping threatened to set off a wave of violence that even the Hombres weren't used to.

The hell of it was that no one would know. Wiseguys did their work quietly. Luke remembered when two Hartford Hispanic gangs fought for territory in a small Connecticut town. For one summer, tensions built between the gangs until one of the gang leaders was killed in a shootout. Then, magically, both gangs were gone from the town with no explanation. Only faint whispers followed with what really happened.

"Go with God, then."

Luke got to his bike and rolled it toward Pez, who was on his phone speaking rapidly in Spanish. Luke couldn't hear the words but he saw the look on Pez's face. The Bridgeport Rojos looked worried.

"He's at the Westfield Rojos clubhouse. You know where that is?"

"As a matter of fact, I do."

"They don't want to give him up."

"Well, that's too bad, isn't it?"

"I hope you have some game, *pendejo*."

"I don't see where I have a choice."

CHAPTER THIRTEEN

Confrontations

Emily started her search for Luke at his apartment. She knew the club liked to have road trips on Saturdays, but she thought she'd try anyway. There was no answer at his door, but she expected that. Still, she couldn't help the twinge of disappointment settling in her chest.

She had no idea how Luke would take the news. A part of her hoped that he'd be happy, but she had to be realistic. Emily and her child would be a responsibility that he did not want.

That was too bad.

Every time except the last two they made love, he was careful. There was even that one time in his apartment that he pulled out before he came, and then declared he'd always take care of her. Well, that went out the window when things got too hot for either one of them to think clearly.

She had no idea which time created their child, either that frantic love making before Gibs was shot, or that time in the funeral home, but neither one of them took measures to prevent a pregnancy. That was on both of them. Luke would just have to step up for his part.

If he didn't want her, she'd live with that. It tore her heart to shreds when she thought of it, but she couldn't make him want her. However, she wasn't going to let him ignore his child. The baby deserved more than that.

The next place she didn't want to go to, but it was necessary. If there was any place that Luke would be after a road trip, it was the Red Bull. She'd never been there, and never expected she would, though she, like every other person who travelled the main drag, would drive right past it.

Her stomach quivered as she stepped out of her car. Time felt like it slowed as she put one foot in front of the other. The door loomed in front of her but she could not bring herself to grab the handle.

"You're overreacting," she told herself. "It's just a bar."

But the problem was that it wasn't just any bar, but the place where Luke hung out. People would know him there and they didn't know her. She had no idea what type of reception she could expect.

The door swung open suddenly, and she jumped back, startled.

"Sorry," said a leather-clad biker. A woman hung off his arm.

"It's okay," said Emily. Screwing up her courage she walked inside. People milled about or sat at booths that lined the walls. In the center was the bar. She walked toward it feeling like she walked as carefully as she would on broken glass. Deciding to sit at the bar, she took an empty stool. A thin, dark-haired man moved quickly from one end of the bar to the other, pouring drinks and handing them off. For some reason, he reminded her of Saks.

"What will you have, miss?"

"A ginger ale."

His eyebrows rose. "Not a drinker."

"Not now."

"Then you waiting on someone?"

"Yeah, I guess you can say that. Has Luke Wade been in tonight?"

The bartender smiled. "Luke? Well, I don't expect him tonight. He's got a shindig going over at his shop. They are opening a new clubhouse he built there."

"Oh," said Emily. "I guess I'm in the wrong place then."

"I wouldn't say that. If you hung around, a looker like you wouldn't be lonely long."

Emily smiled faintly. "Thanks. But I have to go."

"Well, come back any time."

"Thanks." She walked out of the bar more disappointed than ever. There was so much about Luke's life she didn't know anything about. That bartender acted like women asked about Luke all the time, and they probably did. And why wouldn't they. Luke was a handsome man and any woman would want him. She got in her car and sat inside, fighting the tears in her eyes. It's only been three months, but he seemed to have moved on just fine.

Why couldn't she?

She loved him that was why. She'd never been able to move on, not since high school and definitely not now. She hugged her stomach. In her mind she cradled in her arms the reminder of how much she loved Luke. If this child was all she could have of Luke, then that would have to be enough. She knew then that giving this child up was not an option. She was keeping him... or her.

Maybe one day she'd find a way to move on.

But not until after she confronted the bastard who broke her heart.

As she drove from the Red Bull to Luke's shop, she grew more nervous. She'd been to two places already looking for him and came up empty. Now that she knew she was actually going to face him, the tension was giving her a headache and making her anxious.

Her stomach rumbled, and she started to feel sick because she hadn't eaten. Reluctantly, she pulled over to a fast food restaurant and went through the drive-thru for a burger and a soda. Parking in the parking lot she took a bite of her burger and immediately lost her appetite.

"What's wrong, kid," she said, patting her stomach, "don't like hamburgers?"

Her mother had told her and her sister how when she was pregnant what she wanted to eat was different for each child. With Emily she craved fatty foods but with Angela all she wanted was salads.

"Well, you'll have to put up with it. I don't have time or money to get something else. That's something you'll have to get used to, kid. We'll never be a rich family."

Emily's stomach settled as the first sips of her Coke and bites of her burger went down. Gradually she felt better. She could see she'd have to be more careful in her diet from now on. She hadn't seen Luke in three months so she had to be almost through her first trimester. She was going to need to see a doctor and get an OB. She'd have to figure everything out. She could do it on her own, she'd be fine.

Feeling stronger and better than she had in a long time, she started the car.

The last few miles to Luke's shop seemed to take forever. She turned on the radio and the song playing reminded her of her relationship with Luke. The words spoke of a love confused by a lack of communication. It pleaded for the other person to say something so the singer didn't have to guess what was going on. It struck Emily that she was guilty of this. She failed all her life to say or do what she really wanted.

Emily knew instinctively why she'd done this. If she tried to say what she felt, or what she wanted, she got shut down immediately by her parents. Maybe it was, as her mom said, a misguided effort to protect her. But it was wrong, an injustice she felt from her earliest years. What were they afraid of? That she'd turn out like a father she never knew?

She sighed. She was going to stop blaming others and start moving forward on her own.

She wouldn't let what happened to her happen to her child. She'd love everything about him or her, good and bad. She'd love the child enough for two parents, if she had to.

She spied the sign for Luke's shop and turned into the parking lot. Looking around, she saw some people walking toward the back of the building. Emily parked her car and followed them.

People seemed gathered to the left of the building. Long-haired bikers with beards in leather cuts and jackets leaned against a Quonset hut with paper plates of food in hand. Women sat at picnic tables set to the left. Emily looked around but did not see Luke.

She didn't see Saks either, which she thought was strange. Finally, she noticed a man who was with Luke at Gibs' funeral. He tended the fire pit, cutting off pieces from the pig spit-roasted there. Emily grabbed a paper plate and waited in line until she got to the pit.

He looked at her with surprise. "Emily? What're you doing here?"

"I'm looking for Luke."

"He's not here."

"But I was told—"

The man took the plate from her hand roughly and leaned toward her.

"You NEED to leave."

"Why?"

"Because Luke doesn't want you here," the man hissed. "Now leave, before I make you."

"I need to speak to Luke," said Emily angrily. "I'm not leaving—"

"What's going on here?" asked a rough voice behind her. He stepped around so Emily could see him.

"An uninvited guest, Aces."

The large man's eyes traveled over her body licentiously. She didn't like the looks of him with his scraggily hair and beard. The patches on his leather vest looked nasty too.

"I don't know, Pepper. She looks pretty inviting to me."

"I think I'll leave now," Emily said, feeling a prickling sensation at the back of her neck. She understood what Pepper was trying to warn her about a moment earlier. Aces was trouble. A bigger, badder version of Evan.

"Don't go. I'd like to get to know you better."

"Aces," said Pepper in a desperate voice, "Luke won't like it. He used to go with her."

"Well, the operative words are 'used to' aren't they, Pepper?"

"Listen," said Emily, hating the fear trembling inside of her. "I just need to talk to Luke. I'll come by the shop later." She tried to move past Aces.

He grabbed her arm roughly. "I say, you're staying."

She wrenched her arm out of his grasp just as the sound of Harleys rumbled into the parking lot. Everyone turned to the sound. Ten Hispanic men and bikes streamed through the gate.

"Fuck!" called Aces. "Rojos! Everyone, get into the clubhouse."

Pepper grabbed Emily's hand and ran with her to the clubhouse. He pulled a chair out for her to sit on. The room was dark, lit only by blue neon spots that washed the curved walls. More light came from the bar, lit overhead by a row of modern black track lights that shown into the mirrored wall. Glass shelves where hung across the front of the mirror that held various bottles of liquor. Further into the room were three pool tables and a huge painting of the Hades' Spawn club patch. Only, it was different from what Emily saw before.

Pepper looked out the door. Two other men crowded next to him with guns in their hands.

"What's going on, Pepper?"

"Aces is talking to them."

"Fuck you!" called Aces and the men on bikes drew their guns. He turned and ran into the building, breathing hard. "Shut the fucking door!"

"What's going on, Aces?" said Pepper.

"Fucking Rojos! That's Waterbury and Westfield out there. They've got Saks, and they say they'll kill him if we don't back off."

"Fuck them!" said one of the other men. "What do we care? He left the club."

"My sentiments, Dagger," said the other guy holding a gun. "But we can't let them disrespect the club, and right now that's what they are doing."

"We won't," said Aces grimly. "Ladies, get to the back of the club behind the pool tables, and whatever you do, keep your heads down. You, you, you, and you," Aces said, pointing to some other bikers as the women moved to the back of the clubhouse. "Go out the back, circle around and cover the flanks. Dagger and Flint," he said, pointing to two others, get to the roof and give us some cover. We're going to give these fuckers a lesson they'll never forget."

Aces stopped and looked at Emily. "What are you waiting for, sweetheart? Bullets are going to start flying any minute. You don't want to be in the fucking line of fire. Get your pretty ass over by the pool tables!"

Emily winced as he spoke to her. She knew she was in shock. It felt like being rocketed back to Gibs' house only months before. She couldn't move.

Pepper ran over and pulled her to her feet, pushing her toward the other women. "Keep your head down, Emily. This isn't a joke."

CHAPTER FOURTEEN

Rescue

As their bikes rumbled down the highway, four more bikers from Pez's club joined them. Luke could only assume they came at Pez's call, maybe from the one that was made before they left the Red Bull.

Luke signaled with his hand the right-hand turn at a rest stop off the highway. He traveled down the winding service road to the rest stop. There were only a couple cars so Luke let his bike idle.

"What are we doing here, *pendejo*?" asked Pez over the roar of his engine.

"The Westfield club's land starts just over that hill." Luke pointed at a section of trees to the left. "I thought it would be a good idea to have a couple people come up from behind."

Pez nodded his head.

"Good idea. So what do we do?"

"Just follow that trail, but be careful. They use it themselves for the bathrooms in the rest area."

"Wow!" Pez said sarcastically. "They're living like rich bitches here, aren't they?"

"You put twenty guys in a trailer and you'd be more than happy to take a walk."

"I suppose, *ese*. Okay, Jorge, Speed, Chigger, go onto the back part and draw up close to the trailer."

Luke shook his head, wary of what they were about to do but knowing they had no choice but to work together. "They'll have their bikes at the back of the trailer at the base of the hill. The trailer is on the top of the hill so they have good eyeballs all around the place. Keep an eye for lookouts."

"We ain't idiots, *blanco*," snapped one of the Rojos.

"Shut your trap, Jorge," warned Pez. "He didn't have to come here. It ain't his business, except the guy they have is his friend. Keep ears on this one."

Jorge grumbled, but he and the others parked their bikes.

"Tig," said Pez to the last Rojos, "watch the damn bikes."

"No, Pez, I'll—"

"Do what you're damn told, *cabron*. You ain't a patched member yet. You stay here, keep your head down and make sure no one messes with the bikes."

Tig crossed his arms, then finally sighed and nodded his head.

"Okay," said Luke. "I'll go up the main entrance and keep them distracted."

"You ain't going alone," said Pez, revving his engine. "I've got my orders."

"I can't stop you." Luke bent back and opened his saddle bag. He pulled out his leather cut that Aces gave to him with the new patches at the beginning of the summer, and slipped it on.

"You looking for trouble?" said Pez, staring at it.

"Nope, trouble found me. I might as well look the part." He tied back a black bandana on his head, and put on his sunglasses. "Let's go. Clock's ticking."

"Yeah. I got that, man. Otherwise, the war of the century will start without us."

"You don't know the half of it."

Luke charged up the washed out gravel drive leading to the local Rojos clubhouse. He didn't try to hide his entrance onto Rojos land because that would be useless. With the way they sent out the picture of Saks, they'd be expecting someone to show up.

They just didn't expect it to be him.

Luke stopped a hundred yards from the clubhouse. It seemed curiously deserted. Unlike the last time, no one stirred at the window. The front door hung open carelessly.

Pez drove up next to him and they both stared at the ramshackle trailer.

"No one looks to be home," said Luke. "Did someone lie to you, Pez?"

"Not me, *pendejo*. That would rain a world of hurt on them." He cleared his throat and then shouted, "Hey! *Cabrons*. Get your sorry asses out of that trailer."

Awkward seconds passed and nothing happened.

Luke put down his kickstand.

"What do you think you're doing, *pendejo*?" growled Pez. "Stay on that bike!" Pez drew out a handgun from his back and shot into the sky. The sound cracked through the sweltering early evening air. Crows flew, squawking from the tree line on either side of the wide swath of grassy land where the trailer squatted. "Hey! Assholes. Get out here now. This is direct from Lil' Ricki!"

Luke gave a quick glance to Pez. He had guessed Pez was a representative of someone in state leadership, but he hadn't suspected the incarcerated head of the Rojos.

The door swung open and the hang around who had knifed Luke came out looking terrified.

Pez stared hard at the young twenty-something. "Whatchyer name?"

"Ocho."

"Well, Ocho, where's your membership?"

The young man swallowed hard and glanced at Luke. "They went to crash the Spawn party."

"What!" Pez spit a steady stream of obscenities.

"Where's my brother?" Luke set his kickstand down and swung off the bike, making sure the bike wouldn't sink into the ground before he let go of it.

"In the trailer."

"Better be," warned Pez.

But before Luke could get two paces, a shot fired, landing in front of his feet. Dirt and gravel sprayed upward.

Luke instinctually hit the dirt and Pez jumped off his bike seeking cover behind Luke's. Pez shot off several rounds toward his left where the shots seemed to come from.

The front door of the trailer flew open and a white-haired old man stood there with a gun to Saks' head. Bloodied and bruised, Saks looked like crap as the older man gripped his neck.

Pez stood and leveled his gun at the old man.

"*Sarmanbiche* Wizard," he spat. "We knew you were behind this shit."

Luke shook his head. What the hell was going on? He huffed. He'd had enough of this shit. "If he is," hissed Luke, "he's a police informant."

"How do you know?"

"My man Gibs was arrested on an anonymous tip just after he picked up a package from Wizard."

"You can't believe that shit," yelled Wizard, pressing the gun closer to Saks' temple.

"I don't know, *pendejo*. I think it takes one to know one."

Wizard's eyes moved wildly back and forth.

"Let the *blanco* go, Wizard." Pez kept his voice low, but the warning was clear.

Wizard jerked Saks' head hard, pushing the gun behind his ear. "These assholes are responsible for my son's death."

"Now, that's on you, *ese*, sending boys to do a man's job. Don't think that Lil' Ricki doesn't know you are the *cabron* who sent those boys to take a hit out on Spade here. Something he's forbidden. Now you've kidnapped a member of a Wiseguy family for what?" Pez stood, his arms folded over his chest. He wasn't scared of Wizard.

"I didn't know nothing about this guy's family. He's a Spawn and the Spawn are messing in our business."

"*Estupido*! Only because you let them."

"You can't prove anything!"

"So what? This ain't no fucking law court."

Another gunshot split the air, this time hitting Luke's Sportster.

"What the fuck? Hey!" shouted Luke.

More gunfire crackled, this time coming from behind the trailer and a man fell from a position on a tree limb.

"Who the fuck was that?" yelled Wizard, his gun pressed into Saks' neck. The click of the safety clearing echoed across the drive.

"Rojos' justice. Give it up now, Wizard," said Pez, walking toward the trailer. "You're outnumbered and outgunned. You ain't living through this if that man in your hand dies."

Wizard jerked his head around, first toward Luke, then to the back of the trailer. With a rough shove he tossed Saks through the door to the ground. Saks landed with a thud and moaned as Luke rushed forward. Wizard disappeared into the depths of the trailer.

Luke pulled Saks away from the door but stayed flush with the trailer, using what he could as cover.

"You! *Estupido*, in the trees. Toss down your gun and get over here. Now!"

A man dropped a weapon and then hit the grass, but instead of making toward Pez, he tore off into the thick tree line. One of Pez's men disappeared after him.

A scuffle literally rocked the trailer and then Wizard was tossed out the front door and landed at Pez's feet. Jorge and Speed jumped out of the trailer and hauled the man to his feet.

"What do we do with him, boss?" said Jorge.

"Tie him to that fucking chair he put the *blanco* on. His presidente will be here soon to deal with him."

Wizard started struggling.

"No man, you can't—"

"Estupido," hissed Pez. "You think the Rojos and the Hombres don't think the same on this? We're brothers, something you've forgotten."

Pez turned his back on Wizard.

"Gag him when you tie him up. No need to listen to him beg like the *pendejo* he is until his leadership shows. And when they do, find me. You don't need to be part of that shit."

"Si, homes," they said at the same time.

Pez squatted next to Luke and Saks. "Can he ride?"

Saks opened a swollen eye. "Hell, I can always ride."

"Let's go then. Your *familia* is waiting on you."

"Oh, fuck," muttered Saks.

Luke helped Saks to his bike and after he swung on, he helped his buddy on the back. He worried Saks would fall off as they rode, but Saks clung to him as they raced toward the Red Bull. When they arrived there were few bikes and, strangely, a lot of cars in the parking lot.

As he slipped off Luke's bike, Saks took a moment to steady himself. He stared at the line of cars. "Why the fuck did you involve them, Luke?"

"I didn't. Your cousins did."

Saks groaned. "I'll never hear the fucking end of this."

"Whatcha complaining about, *blanco*?" said Pez cheerily. "We saved your ass, didn't we?"

"You don't want to know what stirring this hornet's nest is like. There'll be fighting for weeks about what we're going to do about those Spics." Saks touched the swelling around his eye gingerly.

Pez's face flushed.

Saks realized his mistake. "Sorry, man. Nothing against you. It's just that's how they think."

"Yeah, I get that, *blanco*. Your people had a bunch of business sewn up until the Feds started taking down their organization."

Saks laughed. "Oh, they aren't down. Not by a long shot. Just more underground. I always stayed away from the business," he said, and sighed before he continued, "but you can't stay away from family."

"Well, if you don't get in there, they won't be staying away from us."

Saks nodded. "Yeah. You coming in?"

"No, *blanco*," said Pez. "I've got other business tonight. We're just waiting on my crew to show up."

"Luke?" Saks turned to his buddy.

"Can't, sorry." He shook his head. "Go, say hello to your family for me." He revved the engine and then let it idle. "Oh, and Saks? Take a few days off work too."

Saks blinked in surprise. "Are you sure? I'll be fine by Monday."

"Yeah, I'm sure. There's shit going down. Best you stay away. Your family would appreciate that."

Saks nodded grimly. "Yeah. They always ruin my fun. Hey, Luke?"

"Yeah?"

"Thanks."

"Sure."

"Thanks to you, too." Saks held his hand out to Pez, who bumped his fist into his palm.

"Keep your *familia* calm."

Saks turned and walked into the Red Bull.

"You know," said Luke. "I talked to Sal, the presidente of the Rojos here in Westfield."

"Yeah, *ese*, I know. He called me after you spoke to him."

That bit of news knocked back Luke. "What? Did you send him to me?"

"Yeah, I told him to tell you to back off, that we'd handle our problem."

"That's not how it worked out."

"It would've if it wasn't for Wizard trying to off you." Pez spit at the ground. "Wizard's been holed up in Westfield trying to avoid us. He heard your whole conversation with Sal. You see, Sal was Wizard's kid and Sal denied up and down that his dad was staying with him." He lit a cigarette and offered one to Luke.

Luke took the cigarette and lit it as the sun began to sink behind the trees. "Fuck. And I asked him to turn in his father."

Pez shrugged. "I think until then, Sal didn't know how fucked up his old man had screwed things. Wizard lies real good. That *sarmanbiche* talked out one side of his mouth with your president. He also had Sal believing that Lil' Ricki wanted to cut the Rojos out of the business. At first we thought the Spawn were just playing badass. They aren't no threat. But with the new talent you have in your club, you *pendejos* can fuck things up good. That's why I was sent here, *ese*, to straighten this shit out."

A cold chill went up Luke's spine. Now he understood why Pez declared Luke's property neutral ground. Pez probably had a good idea what was going to go down tonight. He created uncrossable ground that would damn the Rojos trampling on it now. No one statewide, Rojos or Hombres, would sympathize with what would happen to them this day.

"You don't intend to let anyone walk off my property, do you?" Luke said coldly.

"Only you, *pendejo*. Lil' Ricki wants you for himself."

CHAPTER FIFTEEN

Under Fire

Emily's heart beat furiously against her chest as she stared at Aces giving orders to the men and women in the clubhouse. He paid no more attention to her as he peered outside through the window by the door.

Suddenly the lights cut out, with only the fading evening light spilling through skylights in the ceiling and the windows on either side of the door. The room was in semi darkness.

"Fuck," bitched a woman. "There's no signal on my phone."

"Shut your trap," Aces spat. "Fuckers are using a jammer."

"What're you going to do?" breathed Emily, moving closer to try and see outside a window. She knew she shouldn't. It could be stupid dangerous, and yet she had to see what was going on outside. What if Luke was out there?

"You still here, sexy lady? I told you to get to the back of the clubhouse."

"I'm not—"

"Do you think I fucking care, bitch?" he shouted. "Now move!"

Emily swallowed hard and took a step back. A bullet struck the front window, cracking it in a spider web pattern. A rough hand grabbed her arm and pulled her down.

"Crawl," snarled Aces. "If they catch any movement again, that window will be shot out. I don't have fucking time to deal with dead people or some bitch's injuries."

Emily dropped to her hands and crawled to the back of the room.

"Psst, Emily," someone whispered. She whipped her head toward the sound and saw Pepper on his knees inside a doorway. He motioned for her to move toward him.

Looking over her shoulder she saw Hades' Spawn men with their backs to her. Hurriedly she crawled to the doorway. Pepper opened the door wide and urged her inside.

Emily blinked in surprise. It was a small apartment. A camp lantern sat on the middle of the table, beating back the encroaching darkness in the room. The table sat beside a double bed decked out with thick cushions so it could serve as a couch as well. A small galley-sized kitchen extended at the end of the bed with a half wall that had a counter on top of it, just like in her own apartment. "What is this place?" she whispered.

Pepper locked the door. There was no window in the wall, but there was a skylight on one side in the curve of the roof.

"Luke made these apartments for club members. What the fuck are you doing here, Emily?"

"I needed to talk to Luke."

"Really? After he pushed you away?"

"What do you know about it?"

"Not much to know. He stopped seeing you, didn't he?"

"Yeah," she mumbled and then stared Pepper straight in the eyes. "Well, fuck him!"

Pepper stared at her in surprise. "There's a reason he sent you off. Don't you understand? The men in this club don't play nice. They're criminals. Luke was trying to protect you."

"Yeah, sure."

"Emily, I'd never seen a man so wrecked after you left. Whatever he did, he did for your safety, not his."

Emily crossed her arms as she watched Pepper. "Then he's an ass, shoving me away, thinking he was acting all noble and shit. I have a few words for Mr. Luke Wade. He's not going to like it."

Despite the seriousness of the situation around them, Pepper grinned. "Good, you do that."

"I will," she snapped.

"If we get out of here alive."

Emily sat down on the bed and rubbed her temple. "I guess I chose a bad day to tell him off."

"That's an understatement."

"Can't we call the police from here?"

"On our cell phones?" He checked his phone. "Nope. They're using cell jammers that reach here too."

"They can do that?"

"It's illegal. But then again, they aren't the type of men that follow the law, are they?"

"You seem like you don't like them very much. Why're you hanging out with them?"

Pepper turned his attention to the door again. "Aces is getting antsy. Fuck, now he's calling for me. Stay right here. Please. If you hear bullets, get down behind that counter and stay there."

Before Emily could say anything, Pepper hurried out of the door.

Emily hugged herself trying to keep her terror at bay. It all felt like a terrible dream, a nightmare. She'd woken up to go wedding dress shopping, bumped into her awful ex, came home pregnant, had her stupid ex try to claim the baby as his, found out her father wasn't her father, and then went to look for her baby's real father, only to end up in a motorcycle club gun fight. This wasn't a dream, it was a bloody soap opera!

Except it was real. It was happening right now. She cringed as she heard men's whispered shouting below her and above her, men crawling on the roof. Moving to the kitchen, she clutched the countertop for support.

She couldn't die, not now.

"Sorry, baby," she whispered to her unborn child. "I screwed up again." It seemed like in the past four months she couldn't do anything right. Pepper's declaration that they wouldn't make it out alive echoed in her mind. Now her impulsiveness put her and her child in a life-threatening situation.

The minutes ticked on, the quiet in the clubhouse and the scraping sounds of men on the roof jacked her anxiety. Now her terror threatened to grow into a full-blown panic attack and she put her hands over her mouth to keep from hyperventilating. She grew lightheaded, and her stomach reeled. Suddenly the fast food roiled in her stomach, telling her that meal was a monumentally bad idea.

Loneliness and terror closed around her. She didn't want to be here. She didn't know who she was anymore. The revelation that her father wasn't her father left her numb. She couldn't process it right now so she tried to force the thoughts away to deal with later.

It didn't help. She thought about her mother, in the same situation Emily was in now, pregnant, alone, and the father of her baby hanging in the wind. What caused her biological father to reject her mother? It was a question she couldn't answer. The fact that her mother had said her biological father was in prison shook her. What had he done? Worse yet, did Emily inherit his wrongs and would she find herself always making bad decisions?

She swiped at the tears sliding down her cheeks and pushed the thoughts away. She looked around the tidy little room and moved back to the bed, crawling into the corner and sinking into the cushions.

Where was Luke? If he was so hell bent on being with this club instead of her, where was he in this life and death situation? He should be saving her, getting her out of this mess. She wished he would be her knight in shining armour. It was stupid, she knew it, but still...

The creaking of the door caused her to jump. In the gathering gloom of the room darkened by the sinking of the day's sun, she scrunched back into the cushions of the daybed, hoping that whoever entered wouldn't notice her.

"Emily?" hissed Pepper in an urgent whisper.

"Yeah," she whispered back, her voice coming out as a squeak.

He closed the door behind him. "It's just me. Aces is still thinking things over down there. The Rojos have lined up with their bikes, but no one is doing anything yet."

"What're they waiting for?" She wished the room had a window she could look out.

"Not to die, I think. It's serious shit out there. Shots are going to fly. Not sure from which club, but someone will. It's just a question of who."

"Why are you back here? Will they know you're gone?"

"I got sent to check the electrical service box, which I'll pretend to do. But more than likely the electricity was cut off by cutting the line to the clubhouse. I looked out of the window and the security light is still on in the garage in back of the shop, so they didn't hit that."

Emily stared at his profile in the growing darkness. "You seem to know a lot about this stuff."

"Yeah," mumbled Pepper as he moved back toward the door. "How about we get you outta here?"

"How?"

"There's a way out back." He opened the door slightly. "The hallway's dark, so follow me out. Just keep quiet, and stay close, okay?"

Emily nodded her head.

Pepper opened the door all the way and walked stealthily into the hall.

Emily took a deep breath and followed. It seemed to take forever to walk down the length of the hall and the back stairs. There were some doors, probably leading to more rooms like the one she'd been in. Her heart thudded hard against her chest. Pepper opened the back door slightly and muddy light from the moon illuminated the trees outside. He went to step out into the gloom and immediately bullets hit the half-opened door.

Pepper jumped back and pushed Emily back as well. He grabbed her hand and pulled her into the first little room in the hall.

"Shit," he hissed.

Something wet and thick filled her palm. She moved toward the camp lantern and checked her hand. "You're bleeding!" Emily checked his hand where a small river of blood dripped from it.

"Yeah, it burns like a motherfucker." He slipped it behind his back so she wouldn't see it. "Don't worry, it's only a flesh wound."

She ignored his comment. "Where's the bathroom?"

"That door in the kitchen area. There."

Emily moved swiftly and felt around until she found a towel hanging from the bar on the wall. Making her way back through the small apartment she swiftly wrapped the towel around Pepper's hand.

Pounding at the door startled both of them.

"What the fuck? Pepper!"

Pepper went to the door and pulled it open slightly. "Stop fucking yelling," he hissed in a low voice. "I got shot. Give me a minute." He held his hand out the door and the towel that turned red from sopping up his blood. "Tell Aces they got us covered from the back. I can't get out and check the box."

Emily heard some grumbling, but Pepper shut the door.

"Asshole," mumbled Pepper. He held his hand in the air, trying to stop the flow of blood. "Listen, this is my room. I brought my camping gear. There's a first aid kit in the duffle in the closet." He waved his good hand to the folding doors that extended down the right-hand wall.

Emily opened the closet doors to the wide closet and retrieved the duffle and then the first aid kit. "Give me your hand."

Pepper yielded his hand and Emily cleaned the blood the best she could with some wipes in the kit. The bullet that hit him nicked the outer edge of his left hand. "You're going to need to get that looked at. It looks like it's swelling already." She swallowed the bile in her throat, refusing to let herself gag or throw up. She was surprised at how well she managed.

"Yeah, something's broken in there, but we don't have any paramedics around do we? Just put some gauze on it and wind the tape around my palm."

"Where's the tape? I don't see any."

"That blue roll. It's that cohesive shit. It sticks to skin and itself."

"Looks pricey."

"It is. Works great though."

Emily had to agree. The tape was easy to work with, and soon Pepper's hand was bandaged with several thick gauze pads and a layer of the cohesive tape wrapped around his palm.

He flexed his hand and winced.

Emily stared at the man and then to his first aid kit, which had a number of oddly pricey items in it for a general first aid kit. Pepper didn't seem the camping kind, and for a mechanic, even one that ran with outlaw bikers, he seemed too calm and collected for what was going on around him. She swallowed. "I get the feeling you've done this before, Pepper."

"What do you mean?"

"Been in the middle of a shootout. You serve in the armed forces?"

"Yeah," he said grimly. "Afghanistan. Marines. After I got out of high school."

"Then what're you doing with these guys? Other than that 'prospect' patch on your cut, you seem like a nice guy."

"Yeah, I'm a fucking prince."

"No. Don't do that."

"Do what?"

"Look, if I'm going to die, give me some honesty here." She caught her lip, about to tell him she was pregnant with Luke's baby. His annoyed head shake stopped her.

"You don't just fucking give up, do you?" he hissed.

"I wouldn't say that. In fact, I've given up on everything important in my life, especially Luke. But I've had enough of giving up."

He stared at her and then shook his head. "And look where that's got you now."

"Yeah. I suppose that's the meaning of irony, isn't it?"

"Somewhat. Yet, I'm not laughing here."

"You're right. I'm not either. "

"What the fuck you doing in there?" growled someone through the door.

"Hold your dick. I'll be right out." Pepper looked into her eyes. "Go into the bathroom and get in the tub. Shit's about to get very deep."

CHAPTER SIXTEEN

Wiseguys

The click of a gun cocking behind them put both Luke and Pez on alert. Luke's hand went to the gun tucked in the back of his waistband.

"Easy, Spade," said a gravelly voice. Luke recognized the voice of Shelton Rocco, the owner of the Red Bull. He preferred to be called by his nickname though.

"Rock?"

"Yeah. You and the spic come into the bar. We want to talk to you."

"Fuck you," said Pez.

"Shut your mouth. You don't have a choice, asshole."

"My homes will be here soon."

"Yeah. Not a problem. They'll wait out here with some of my family while we talk business. Move!"

"Come on, Pez." Luke kicked down the stand and turned off the motor.

Warily, Pez eyed Rock and dismounted his bike. He followed Luke into the bar, Rocco followed with his gun trained on them. Luke noticed shapes of men standing by the back edge of the bar, watching the entrance to the parking lot of the bar.

Pez muttered under his breath.

"Shut your mouth," warned Rock.

The inside of the bar was dark and thick with cigarette and cigar smoke. Rocco locked the door after he entered.

"Behind the bar," said Rock.

Luke made his way around the bar to find the tables mashed together in a single row and a bunch of men seated around it.

Many of them were old men with sharp faces and gray hair. The younger ones were no more than in their forties. Saks sat in a booth leaning against the wall.

"Mr. Wade," said an elderly man at the head of the table. He spoke with a thick Italian accent like that language was his first. "I understand that we have you to thank for returning our Anthony."

"Yes, sir," said Luke. "Pez helped too."

The man nodded. "I like that you know the meaning of respect, Mr. Wade. And loyalty. It takes loyalty and courage to do what you did for Anthony. Him, on the other hand," he said, waving his hand toward Pez. "He should be involved. It's his business that brought us to this point, isn't it, Pez?" He spit Pez's name out like it was something disagreeable in his mouth.

Pez stared around the room and drew himself up as tall as he could. Luke shook his head. Getting macho wasn't going to win him points with this crew.

"What of it, old man? As you said, it's our business."

Rock stepped out of the shadows and spun Pez around and socked him in the gut. Pez grunted and doubled over, and the man turned Pez back toward the men at the table.

"You don't know the meaning of respect, Spic, and that's the problem. This territory was ours long before your kind showed up and it will be ours long after you are gone. Capisci?"

"Don't you mean capisce?" sneered Pez.

"Stunata!" The men at the table laughed.

"You're crazy, Spic, to stand here at this table acting like an asshole. We're going to decide what to do about you and the rest of you. Our interests don't conflict, but causing trouble with people like Mr. Wade makes law enforcement pick up their ears, making it hard for us to operate."

"What're you going to do about it, eh, *ese*? Your kind is nothing here anymore."

The man hit his hand on the table hard, making drinks set on it jump. "Stupido! We're fucking everywhere! And we got people ready to come into the state and take care of you and your associates. It will cost us some money, but we'll do it to make sure you don't fuck things up anymore than you have."

Luke stood stock still, barely breathing. It was true that people believed Wiseguys' influence had diminished, but incidents reported in the local news said otherwise. There had been too many mysterious and unsolved deaths in the past couple years, deaths connected with the businesses Wiseguys were supposed to control. Now these men were going to decide what to do about the Rojos? What was worse, they thought they could do it too.

"We'd just rather avoid spending the money. So what are you going to do to make sure our cost of doing business remains low, *ese*?" The last word came out in a hiss.

The man spoke with such menace that Luke wondered what they were doing here still standing.

"What do you want?" Pez stared into the old man's eyes, still unafraid.

The man glanced around the table to different men there. Some of them gave a nod. Luke got the feeling they talked this subject over quite a bit before they got here.

"One. You'll knock off the social biker clubs. We don't like them, but from time to time they provide a useful diversion for the cops' interest."

"We don't care about them anyway."

"Bullshit! If you didn't show an interest in Mr. Wade's club we wouldn't be here."

"That's on their president."

"We know about that asshole. Hard to ignore him. But it takes two to say yes, and someone in your club said yes."

"We've taken care of him."

"You sure about that, Spic?"

Pez shrugged. "We sent enough of a message."

"You better be sure about that. I'm holding you personally responsible for keeping a lid on that shit."

"You aren't telling me anything I don't know."

"Two. You're to give us a cut of the club's profits."

Pez laughed then. "Ask for the moon. You are likely to get that first."

Rock grabbed Pez's shoulder to turn him toward him again, but the man at the head of the table waved him off. "You don't seem to understand. This isn't a negotiation. I've got people more than willing to take over your business, Spic. You've got to make it worth our while not to do that."

"You aren't interested in the drug business. Too high risk."

The old man spread his hands. "True, we backed off and let the blacks and spics take the majority of the business. But times are tough. Revenue streams have dried up. But we can make things worth your while. We've got people on the payroll that can make things easier for you. But hey, your choice."

"I'm going to have to take this to leadership, man. I'm just a mouthpiece."

"Oh, I doubt that. But you want to confer with your associates, go ahead. You've got twenty-four hours. Now get out of here."

Rock wasted no time in shepherding Pez toward the door. Luke couldn't believe what he was hearing. It felt like he had been punched in the gut. They were just going to let Pez go? What about his club, the people on his property right now threatened by the Westfield Rojos?

"Wait!" said Luke. "That's it?"

"Yes, Mr. Wade. Now, if you know what's in your best interests you won't repeat any of this conversation to anyone."

"But my shop, my club."

"Sadly, collateral damage," the Italian elderly man said, holding out his hands.

There was a knock at the back door, and someone moved off to answer it.

"You can't let that happen!" Luke said as a tall man moved toward the elderly man. So intent was Luke on his conversation he didn't realize who it was until he spoke.

"I'm afraid he's right, Pops."

Luke stared in shock at Detective Anglotti standing in back of the man. "I've been pushing into the Fed's investigation, just as you wanted. And this man here, his name isn't Luke Wade. It's Icherra, Raymondo Icherra."

The elderly man stared at Luke appraisingly.

"A spic. But not just any spic. What's your connection with the Icherras?"

"I was named after my uncle," mumbled Luke, trying to hold the anger burning inside of him.

"Migna!" swore the old man. The other men at the table started muttering.

"Worse yet, Pops, word is that a couple of his uncles' men landed at Bradley a few hours ago."

"You!" said Pops, pointing to Pez at the front door. "What do you know about this?"

Pez gave a grin as evil as a jack-o'-lantern in the dark. "There's a reward for information on a man with a mother from Hispaniola, and a father from Mexico. Seems like, *ese*, your uncle's been looking for you for a long time. My people know I was with you and they know where I am now."

I'm fuckin' dead. Luke rubbed his temple.

Pez turned his head toward the elderly man. "Now, old man, who is in what shit?"

Everyone at the table started speaking at once.

"Silence! Tie that shithead up right now!" he spit, pointing to Pez. "And you, Wade, or Icherra, or whatever the hell your name is. You better start talking now. Why are your uncle's men here now?"

Luke stared at the man, feeling a frisson of fear settle in his gut. What should he tell him? He looked over to Anglotti, who stared at him with menace. If the corrupt detective didn't have the whole story, he could find it out. Luke decided the best thing was to tell the truth.

"I don't know. I haven't seen my uncle since I was five. My father and mother moved to the United States after that. I was too young to know what was going on. Later, I found out we were in Witsec. Both my parents were killed when I was eight, and the program put me here in Connecticut with a foster family. I had several until I graduated high school. Then I was cut loose. Or so I thought." No use in hiding the story anymore. It didn't matter. He was so glad he'd cut Emily loose from this hell. At least she would be safe.

"And you never had contact with your uncle?"

"Nope."

"I don't think that matters, Pops," said Anglotti. "Icherra's only son was killed last year. He may be looking for Luke to take his place in the family. In any case, Icherra's not going to be pleased if anything happens to this guy or his."

"His?" said Luke. "What do you mean by that?"

"Your girlfriend, Emily, is in your clubhouse right now," sneered Anglotti.

"What?"

"We've been doing surveillance on your shop, and your clubhouse. One of our guys saw her enter a few hours ago. She hasn't come out." Anglotti smiled smugly.

Luke started for the door and was pulled back by Rock.

"Let me go!" He struggled and several men at the table rose and grabbed him.

"What do you think you're going to do, Spade, eh?" said Rocco as Luke twisted, trying to break their grip.

"I've got to get her out of there!"

"Hey, we understand your worry, Spade, but walking in there is as good as getting killed."

"No," said the old man, cutting through the chaos. Everyone else stopped speaking. "Let him go."

Hands fell away, and instantly Luke was free.

"Go. See what you can do. We appreciate what you did for Anthony. Go with God."

Luke thought it was incongruous that this man would invoke God's name, but he wasn't going to argue. "What about Pez?"

"He'll remain our guest until we get some things straightened out."

Luke nodded, knowing better than to argue. He walked out of the Red Bull and into the night with his heart racing. What the hell was Emily doing at the clubhouse? He sped to his bike and ignored the other Rojos sitting on their bikes, hands up, looking at the men half in the shadows pointing weapons at them.

He jumped on his speedster and started it. He had no illusions about why the crime boss let him go. If Luke got killed in a confrontation with the Rojos, then the Hispanic gang would be the ones to earn his uncle's wrath. Mexican drug cartels were utterly ruthless and took no prisoners. The Wiseguys would do anything to avoid a war with them.

All heads in the parking lot turned to him, but he didn't care. He had to get to Emily. He couldn't let anything happen to her. It would kill him if he did.

So either way he was a dead man.

CHAPTER SEVENTEEN

Under Siege

Emily cowered in the small shower, once again alone with her thoughts. If Pepper, who had at least some military training, couldn't see a way out of here, what was she supposed to do?

Dear God, please, please, please get us out of here alive.

She felt bad about her furtive prayer. What did she do to earn God's attention? Nothing but break every commandment she felt like breaking.

The front door opened and closed again as Emily pressed against the shower. Had Pepper returned? Or was it one of the other club members checking out why Pepper was in and out of here so much?

"Hey, Emily?"

Emily released a sigh of relief at the sound of Pepper's voice. "What's going on?"

"Aces wanted to know where Luke was."

Emily wondered the same thing. "Do you know?"

"All I know is that he went to Saks' apartment to see what he could find out. Saks had been missing since sometime after work yesterday."

"Shouldn't Luke have returned by now?"

"I think so, but maybe..."

"Maybe? Maybe what?"

"Where's George?" muttered Pepper. He stared at the wall as if it had answers.

"Pepper, who's George?"

Pepper sighed. "My partner, or supposed to be, anyway. Maybe he got Luke out and away."

"Your partner?"

Pepper stared at her, a look that had frustration and regret mixed in, like he failed at something. "I need to get you out of here too."

"I got myself in this mess."

"We made promises to Luke to keep you out of this, so it's my job."

His job? "You're just a mechanic, Pepper." She didn't understand what he was saying.

"After what Luke taught me, I suppose I am." He chuckled and quickly made his face serious when Emily didn't smile. "I'm a DEA agent."

"A cop?" Why in the world was Luke working with the police?

Pepper nodded. "That's how I know Luke didn't want you here. He made a deal to work with us in exchange for keeping you safe."

"You're kinda doing a lousy job." She tried to smile but her lips trembled.

Pepper scratched the back of his neck with his good hand. "Can't argue with you there. I did get your legal charges dropped – as per Luke's requirement."

Emily's hands flew to her lips. "He did that? For me?"

"Yes."

Emily smiled and then her eyes narrowed. "Why are you telling me this?"

"Because I'm the worst undercover ever. I can't see Luke as a bad guy even if my bosses do. After this, if I live and don't get arrested or fired, I'm turning in my shield. I figure I'll live longer that way." Pepper pulled out his dead cell phone and stared at it, then shook his head.

"That your backup?"

"Supposed to be."

"Where are they?"

"Right now? Since my tracker signal went dead, I expect they're calling up a SWAT team and doing calculations."

"Calculations?"

"For the casualties."

Her ears rang. She didn't want the answer to her question, but she asked it anyway. "What does that mean?"

"Well, you do the math. There are ten Hades' Spawn with guns holed up in a clubhouse and ten, or more, Rojos with guns on the outside. Eight women in the clubhouse with no weapons at all. What do you think is the likelihood we're getting out of this with our hides?"

As if to answer for her, the pop, pop, pop of gunfire sounded faintly in the inner walls of the small bath. Cheers and noises of celebration rang through the clubhouse.

Pepper ran out of the bathroom, holding the bloody towel, and Emily followed close behind. She peered down the hall to see a man she did not recognize stand in the middle of a group of Spawn men. They were obviously happy to see him.

"Yeah," bragged the man. "I popped that Rojos good. When I came in the back door I saw his brothers drag him off."

"One down," said Aces. "Nine to go."

"George, man, where have you been," said Pepper. He put his hand loosely wrapped in the towel on George's shoulder.

"When I saw those Rojos come in I took off for the woods, but I came back around and barged through." He grinned. "Who's the man?" He pounded his chest.

"You're bleeding," observed Pepper. "I've got a first aid kit in my room."

"You do?" said Aces, his eyebrows arching. "Good. We may need that."

"That's fine. Let me take care of George first."

Aces waved his hand dismissively and Pepper steered George to the little apartment. George was a slightly pudgy man with dark brown hair and hazel eyes. There appeared to be nothing remarkable about him, which is why, Emily supposed, he'd be good at undercover work. Pepper closed the door once he and George were in the room. He pointed immediately to Emily.

"George, Emily. Emily, George."

"Fuck," said George, staring at the wet blood Pepper transferred from the towel. "You ruined my shirt!"

"Shut up. Where did you go?"

"I made a report to the boss. He said to hang tight, and he'd get a—" he looked at Emily nervously, "team here."

Pepper nodded his head toward her. "She knows."

"You told her? What the fuck?"

"Had to. Kind of in a tight situation here."

"What the hell were you thinking?" George glared at Emily like it was her fault.

Pepper ignored his question. "Is there any chance we can make a run for it? We need to get her out of here."

"One of us would have to lay down cover fire. I'm sure someone else has taken up the position in the tree."

"Strange. And the guys on the roof didn't see it?"

"It's getting dark out there and the position's well camouflaged by the trees."

"You need to tell Aces what you've seen. Maybe we can get him to tell the guys on the roof to shoot at the position and we can get out of here. I'll come with you. Emily, you stay here." Pepper pushed George toward the door and didn't wait for her to reply.

She watched them leave and shuddered at the sudden silence in the room. If she made it through this, she was going to need a month to process all the information inside her brain. She should be terrified, and she was, but for some reason, probably shock, she seemed relatively calm. She was oddly comforted that there were police on the inside. It made her feel protected.

They needed to find a way out.

She moved to the door and pressed her ear against it. She could hear talking and more men were heading down the hall to check the back door, or possibly coming back to the main room. She held her breath, trying to make out what they were saying as they were speaking in low voices and she couldn't tell who was speaking.

"They haven't made a move. What the hell?"

"They're waiting for back-up, for more Rojos." This voice was gruff and Emily assumed it was Aces speaking. "Otherwise they've no advantage."

"Like hell, they're outside, we're trapped in here."

"Fuck look, there's a police car out there."

"What the—? Look! That fucker Ramses is talking and laughing with the pig."

"Who's Ramses?"

"Their vice-prez. He's running things since Sal got shot."

"Asswipe! He probably convinced the guy they were just shooting off rounds for fun."

"Fuck! He's giving him a plate of our pig."

"I should shoot him for that."

"I'd like some more of that pig."

"Shut the fuck up! Stop thinking about your stomach."

There was a moment of silence and then the conversation picked up again.

"The cop's moving off."

"Damn. We could use some police intervention now."

"Shut your pie hole. We don't want cops here, now or ever."

"I just thought of something." It was Aces speaking here. "The other Rojos aren't here yet. That's telling us something."

"How so?"

"Means they have no support for this action."

"So should we start shooting our way out?"

"I think," said Pepper, Emily could her his voice, "their weakest defensive point is the back of the building. If we lay down cover fire, we can get out of here."

"And leave our bikes?"

"Do you want to be alive to ride another day, or do you want to die for your bike?"

"I think—"

"Shut up, dumbass! I don't care what you think." Aces' voice grew louder. "It doesn't pay to have a twenty thousand-dollar bike if your family's spending twenty thousand to put you in the ground."

Someone grunted. "Then what's the plan, Aces?"

"I like Pepper's idea. We'll shoot our way out the back. I'm not being held up in my own clubhouse. This is bull sh—"

"We should get the women out of here first," said Pepper.

"Yeah, hoes before bros in this case. They won't shoot the hoes." Aces cleared his throat. "Listen up. When I give the word, Pepper go get the ladies and lead them out the back way. Tell them to run and keep running."

Emily heard footsteps and more muffled talking. A few moments later she heard the women in the hall and Pepper talking to them.

"Look, it's that or wait for them to hit," said Pepper. "It's better if you get out now. The situation isn't going to improve."

Emily grabbed the door handle and moved to the hallway. She checked her watch. What felt like forever had only been about an hour. It was crazy. "I'll go first," she offered.

"Come on, ladies." Pepper pulled a gun from his waistband and released the safety. The ladies came out of the main clubhouse and lined up in the hall. They all looked terrified.

"George, you lead the way."

"Sure, Pepper."

George walked into the murky depths of the hallway, and Pepper followed.

"Why," whispered Emily to Pepper as she fell in step beside him, "is George going first?"

"Bullet proof vest," Pepper whispered back. "I didn't want Aces to see it and get suspicious."

Other women gathered in back of Emily, the scent of perfume, hairspray and fear permeating the air. Emily was pretty sure she smelled the same as them.

"Back against the wall, ladies," said Pepper, his voice taking on an authoritative tone, "until I tell you to move."

"On three," whispered George. "One, two, three."

Both Pepper and George kicked the back door open, sending it flying, and simultaneously started shooting. Several gunshots flew, pinging the door and the back of the building.

"Down, down, hit the ground," yelled Pepper as he and George fell to the floor and through the opened door furiously returned fire.

"It's coming from all angles," yelled George.

"They're shit at aiming."

"Yeah, but that many bullets are bound to hit something."

Emily crawled backward, terrified a stray bullet would fly inside the building. They weren't safe where they were. "Get in here," she screamed to the women as she opened the door to the room beside where she'd been hiding earlier. "Hide behind the counters and in the shower. Don't open this door for anyone unless you recognize the voice."

She waved them inside, and the eight women moved, crawling on their hands and knees into the tiny apartment. The door shut.

Emily scooted toward the door next to George and pushed it open, then turned around and scurried on her hands and knees towards Pepper's apartment, who had the only light source she knew of in the now totally dark clubhouse.

"She's got an idea," said Pepper. "You take that apartment and I'll take this one and we'll surprise them when they try to breach the clubhouse."

Emily shuddered. This was more than serious. It was a juggernaut of violence that could only end in bodies. With her heart hammering in her chest, she desperately prayed she wasn't one of them. She scurried into Pepper's apartment just as the shooting stopped.

When Pepper and George stopped shooting the Rojos stopped too. Now there was an ominous silence that hung over the Spawn's clubhouse. In the background, police sirens grew louder and then stopped.

The sound of wood breaking and shouting startled Emily.

She heard Aces scream, "They're in! They're in!"

Pepper scooted into the room and shut and locked the door. He stood with his gun pointing at the door with grim determination. He glanced at Emily. "A couple Rojos just rushed the door. They have guns on Aces and the men in the bar. Aces and his men have guns on them. It's a stand-off."

Emily noticed the earpiece in Pepper's ear. She had a feeling he knew more because someone was feeding him information. She couldn't help it. All of a sudden her quickie dinner threatened to come up. She ran into the bathroom, running into the doorframe as she did so, and she fell on her knees in front of the toilet by the sink, heaving so hard her guts hurt. "Oh fuck, oh fuck," she moaned.

"Stay in that bathroom, Emily," ordered Pepper.

She would, though the smells coming from the toilet made her want to vomit more. Emily sat against the wall, the sour taste in her mouth and the roiling in her stomach made her want to lurch for the porcelain fixture once more. She stood shakily and washed her mouth out with water from the sink.

More gunfire went off, sounding like it came from far away, not inside the clubhouse.

There was a loud slamming noise, which Emily guessed was the back door being shut with force. "What the hell's going on here?"

Luke? Her heart sped up and she rushed out of the bathroom to the living room area.

Pepper cracked open the door and Emily clearly heard his voice clearer now.

"Drop your weapons!"

Even in this ludicrous situation she went giddy knowing he was nearby. And safe. She wanted to burst through the door and into his arms.

A gunshot going off stopped her from moving. It was followed by the sound of guns shooting everywhere, and scuffles. People outside rushed in, she heard shouts and screams of men as they fought. Horrified, Emily could only stare at the door, terrified Luke had been hurt, or worse, shot and left bleeding on the ground. Images of Gibs in Luke's arms made Emily's eyes fill. She shut them tight and buried her head in her hands, trying to make the sounds go away.

More noises of things she couldn't see, bumps against the walls, guns going off, and then shouts and more physical fighting followed by a loud groan as someone fell to the floor by the door.

Then suddenly, as quickly as all the noise started, it ended abruptly. Silence followed for a moment. Emily stared horrified at the door, her hand covering her mouth.

"Emily!" Luke shouted. "Where the fuck is she, Aces?"

He was alive! Pissed off, but he was freakin' alive!

Pepper opened the door all the way. "Here, Luke! She's in here with me."

Luke rushed into the room and grabbed her, holding her so close she couldn't breathe. Then he pushed her away from him, as if her touch burned him. "What the hell are you doing here, Emily? Are you crazy?"

CHAPTER EIGHTEEN

Reunion

Luke allowed himself a moment to hold Emily in his arms and to breathe in her scent. He was still jacked up from the entrance he made diving in through the back door of the clubhouse, dodging bullets while he shot off a few rounds towards his attackers. Holding her only added to his anticipation. He'd missed her so much in the past few months that he felt empty enough that he had nothing left to live for. Now she was in his arms again and his heart expanded as he held her close.

"It's over. We stopped the Rojos," he whispered quietly in her ear, unsure if she even heard him.

"I'll," said Pepper, "just go help Aces." He left them alone, shutting the door behind him.

Luke's happiness at their reunion was short lived. This was the worst possible moment for her to be here. He pushed her away, horrified at the situation in which they were both in. "What the hell are you doing here, Emily? Are you crazy?"

Her eyes fluttered wide with shock and fresh tears, then her jaw set and her eyes narrowed. "I guess," she said angrily, "I didn't expect you'd have a shoot-out at a freakin' pig roast."

"I told you—"

"I remember what you told me, Luke Wade. You told me I was a good fuck. Very sweet of you!" She glared at him before huffing. "You are such a liar! Acting like you didn't care about me at all. Pepper told me what you did. You made a deal with the DEA to make all my legal problems go away. You were no freakin' help."

She was so angry, and as much as he hated to admit, the fire in her turned him on, even when he feared for her life. His pecker, which had been in hibernation, suddenly twitched. *Not fuckin' now!* "I did help you!"

"Not in the way that would help me the most. You pushed me away and acted like I was nothing to you." The hurt in her voice could not be hidden by her anger.

"I needed to keep you safe."

Her cheeks blushed red, and her lower lip trembled. "Yeah, by breaking my heart. Nice play, Mr. Tough Guy." She turned away and covered her face in her hands.

He put his hand on her shoulder and urged her to face him. "Emily, I didn't want to hurt you. But it wasn't safe for you to stay. Look what happened to Gibs! These men are all nasty criminals and killers. There's no telling what harm you'd have to face because of me. Look what happened here today!" This was exactly why he didn't want her around here. How she hadn't been shot or injured... He didn't want to even consider the possibilities.

"I don't care!"

"Emily," he pleaded.

"No, Luke Wade! You had no business making that decision for me. You were deliberately cruel! You made me feel worthless because you didn't want me. You treated me like trash. And I felt even worse because you're the only man I could ever want."

"I'm sorry. I'm so, so sorry." What else could he say? He'd only done it to protect her. They weren't out of the woods yet. Not by a long shot. He thought about the Red Bull and a shudder ran down his spine.

"Sorry don't mean shit! Nothing means anything if you don't love me." She faced him, tears streaming down her face as her hands covered her stomach.

"Emily, please."

"We're not in high school anymore, Luke. This is life, our life. Real life!"

He threw his hands up in the air. What the hell? "Don't you think I know that?" his voice raised in frustration.

"I'm pregnant! With your child."

Now that threw him. Fear, and possibly a morsel of hope, raced through his blood. "H-How," stuttered Luke. "Pregnant?"

"I believe it happens the usual way. It's called sex."

His prick signaled it understood. "Pregnant?" he repeated. He stood there dumbfounded. "I was careful." He knew it wouldn't be someone else's. His gut told him that and instinct made him believe. "Aw shit," said Luke, remembering the last two times they were together. One was because Luke thought he might not see her again and the next was when he was sure he'd never see her again. "I'm sorry."

"Yeah, you should be sorry. So should I."

"Emily, that's not what I mean. You can't stay with me." He ran his fingers through his hair. "What I'm involved in, Emily, you wouldn't be safe."

"I told you, I don't care."

"But a child? Oh, man, I screwed things up good."

"Don't you think for one moment this is all on you!" She was mad and he couldn't blame her. Except... was she angry for a different reason? "You didn't do this all by yourself. We're both adults! I fucked you as much as you did me." She lowered her eyes, as if embarrassed by her crass words. "I always want you."

He couldn't bear the torment on her face. It ripped his soul to shreds. How could he turn her away? He didn't want to, not ever again. If there was one truth in his life, it was that he loved Emily Rose Dougherty, now and until the end of his days.

He raised her chin with his fingers so she had to look him in the eye. Even at this worst possible time he felt pride that she carried his child. At that second he understood what it meant for a woman and a man to be joined, their lives woven around each other so that what happens to one happens just as forcefully to the other. Whether it was happiness, joy, sorrow, or triumph, there would never be a moment when he didn't think about her, what she wanted, or what she thought. She was inalterably his today and for the rest of his life.

"Emily, the truth is, from the first day I saw you in high school, you were the only woman I wanted, truly wanted, in my life. Yes, I was wrong to push you away. I thought I was protecting you, that you would forget me."

"I've never forgotten you."

"And I've never forgotten you. I think I understand now. We were never meant to be apart." Circumstances had tried to prove otherwise but Fate knew it was in their destiny.

She stared at him for a long moment. Whatever was going on in the hut beyond this room didn't matter. Whatever Emily had to tell him would either save him, or kill him. "I paid a price for turning my back on you all those years ago. I'll never do that again." Tears rolled down her face. "I've always loved you."

He looked into her beautiful blue eyes and became lost in them. Luke could see the love she had for him, burning fiercely. She was just inches from him and despite everything, or maybe because of it, he couldn't resist the urge to kiss her. All the months of being without her piled on to this one moment. The only thing he could think of was claiming that small, pouty mouth of hers.

Fuck the danger outside. He needed her right now. Whatever was going on in the clubhouse could be handled by those there.

He crushed his lips against hers, sucking her bottom lip into his mouth, exploding with the taste, want and need of her. Everything about her was perfect. As her pert breasts pressed against his chest, he reached and cupped the round globes of her ass in his hands. She groaned and wrapped one leg around his leg. Emily pushed herself against his leg, her hips moving as she gasped and whimpered. Her breathing sped up as she found his bulge beneath his pants. Emily pressed against it, moaning and calling his name.

He was on fire, every cell of his flesh calling for her skin to be flush to his. His shaft pressed impossibly hard against his jeans and his one thought was to delve into her wet heat. Luke tore at the button at her waistband and pushed down her zipper. He slipped his fingers inside, reaching her mound to the treasure between her legs. She was so wet she coated his fingers thoroughly.

Luke put his fingers on either side of her clit, rubbing the tender folds of her flesh that cradled that sensitive spot. She tensed, her breathing ragged, and whimpered.

"Come for me, baby," he said. With rapid breaths she shuddered, her back arching and her head falling back. He held her tight around her waist with one arm while she trembled and moaned. Luke thought he'd never seen or heard anything sexier.

"Fuck, baby," he whispered. "It's so hot to see you come on my fingers."

He drew his hand up and sucked his little and ring fingers in his mouth, savoring her sweet taste. Luke put his other two fingers to her mouth.

"Taste that baby. See how delicious you are."

She lapped his fingers with her tongue and sucked hard on them. Now it was Luke's turn to moan as he imagined his cock in her mouth as she lashed it with her warm, soft tongue.

As if she could read his mind she dropped to her knees, and worked his jeans until they fell around his ankles. Tugging on his waistband she pulled down his boxers as well, freeing his cock. Luke was so rigidly hard, his cock slapped against his stomach.

The light from the camp lantern struck her glittering eyes as she took his shaft in her hand and wrapped her fingers around it. Her small pale hands almost seemed overpowered by his girth, but she smiled wickedly as she stroked him with her gentle fingers sending shocks of electricity up his spine. Emily palmed the head of his cock, spreading his precum around his shaft.

"Oh fuck, Emily."

"Baby," she murmured. In one swift move she engulfed the head of his cock in her mouth. Her tongue sought the sensitive spot beneath his head and involuntarily he jerked, seeking more of that heat down his cock. Emily took him in further, her soft tongue dancing on his flesh, teasing him, and making him wild for more. He gripped her hair between his fingers, and she tightened both hands around his shaft. She was only going to allow him to go so far, but she sucked in what she could, lightly running her teeth on his shaft. He never felt anything this good, and he knew if it kept on like this he'd come in her mouth.

Luke couldn't stand it anymore. He wanted to be inside her. Gently he backed away, and after pulling her to her feet, backed her up to the bed. With great tenderness he lowered her to the mattress. With a quick pull he yanked her jeans off, revealing her creamy hips in the soft light of the camp lantern. Another pull tugged her panties off and the full scent of her arousal hit him.

"Luke," she whimpered. "I need you."

He fucking needed her. He knelt between her legs, pulling her t-shirt over her head, but leaving Emily's arms encased in the fabric. With one hand he held them above her head, while he pushed her lacy bra above her breasts, attacking her nipples with swipes of his tongue, the taste of her skin driving him beyond reason.

"Luke, please," she pleaded, bucking her hips toward him.

Luke grabbed his shaft and slid the tip up and down between her legs and sunk into her heat. Slickness and softness encased him, assailing his senses, driving him beyond reason. He pushed in and she gasped. That one sound sent his thoughts reeling. This was his. She was his.

Emily meowed, a sexy sound that called to the primal parts of his brain. "More," she gasped.

He pulled back and then took her again, filling her with every inch of him. Every nerve tingled and his skin heated like a flash fire.

"Oh fuck, Luke. Please. Harder." She clenched around him and his breathing sped up as he withdrew and thrust, again and again, his strokes increasing in power, fury and need. She moved with him, jutting her hips to him as he pounded her. In the little room there was only them taking and giving everything they had to each other.

"Oh, Luke," she cried as she broke apart, her body pulsing around him.

Nothing felt this good before, never as good as having the woman he loved urging him to drive himself into her. His stomach tightened, his balls drew up, and the rush that signaled his orgasm burst over him in waves, shooting his seed deep inside her. He was suspended in time and space, every part of him, mind, body and soul captured within this moment when he gave all of himself to this woman.

He collapsed in her arms and kissed her. But this kiss, unlike the others, was tender and sweet, filled with all he felt for her in his heart.

"Emily, I love you. Marry me."

CHAPTER NINETEEN

Double Dealing

There was pounding at the door that brought Emily, with a shock, to their present reality.

"Luke," called Pepper. "You better get out here, man!"

Luke scrambled up, and dressed in a few fluid movements. Emily got up and fixed her bra and top. She found her jeans but could not find her panties. With a few quick jerks she pulled up her jeans. Niceties like panties didn't fit a life and death situation. She found her flats and slipped them on while Luke went to the door.

"What's going on?"

"You fucking won't believe this. They have a hostage."

"What?" Luke flew out of the room and Emily followed close behind. Lights from the adjacent parking lot shot a filtered half glow into the darkened clubhouse. Emily made out Aces, Dagger and Wolf knelt below the windows, peering out. Pepper and another man fell behind Luke and Emily.

"What's going on?" said Luke.

Aces waved him over to the window, and Luke scrunched down and made it to the place Aces indicated. Emily did the same, determined not to let Luke out of her sight. Pepper and the other man followed and fell silently behind them.

Luke glanced at her darkly, but turned his head toward the scene out the window. Emily gasped.

The Rojos lined up their bikes in a row facing the clubhouse. They stood by their bikes, pointing their weapons toward the clubhouse, the light from the streetlamp back lit them and bathed their bare arms from the left. The right side of each man, the garage blocking the light, was dark. Emily thought she'd never seen anything as fierce or dangerous as those men in their denim cuts, long hair and bandanas, ready to kill at a moment's notice or even a slip of a finger.

But what was worse, held by the back of his neck, Evan Waters was suspended from the grip of the biggest of them. His face was twisted in terror as the man shook him like a rag doll.

"Evan!" she gasped.

"Who the hell is that guy?" spit Aces.

"A total idiot," said Luke.

"If you don't come out here, Kinney, I'm going to snap this man's neck."

"Go ahead," shouted Kinney. "He don't mean nothing to me."

"No!" said Emily. Whatever happened, no matter how much of a jerk Evan was, he didn't deserve to die at the hands of these men.

Luke stared at Emily, who appealed to him with her eyes not to let Evan's death rest on her head.

He sighed. "Wait!" called Luke.

"What are you doing, Spade," growled Aces.

"I'm going to talk to that man."

"Ramses won't listen to you. There is only one thing he wants, and that is me dead."

"We have his two guys here, and I saw our men on the side of the building and on the roof. So far all we have are minor casualties. If we shoot it out people are going to die. But he can't back down because he's a dick. So I'll see if I can give him a reason to walk away."

Aces scrubbed his face with his hand. "Fuck! Whatever, Spade. See what you can do."

Emily put her hand to her face, afraid of what she would say. She didn't want Luke to go out there but she didn't want to see Evan die. She grabbed Luke's arm.

"Be careful," she pleaded. "We need you."

He nodded and stood.

"I'm coming out! Unarmed!" shouted Luke. He nodded toward Dagger, who opened the door. Luke held up his hands and took the three steps to the blacktop.

Emily watched, her insides clenched tight with fear.

"Who're you?" demanded Ramses.

"The road captain of Hades' Spawn."

Ramses spit on the ground. "Fuck you."

With that, two of the Rojos dropped their weapons and moved, grabbing Luke on either side. He struggled between them but they held tight like he was in a vise.

"What the fuck is this, Aces? Your road captain? You chicken shit bastard!" Ramses shook with anger. "Screw you! Get out here." He dropped Evan to the ground and kicked him viciously. Evan cried out and rolled on the ground.

"Leave him the fuck alone, Ramses. He has nothing to do with this!" Luke hissed.

"The pendejo came around here insisting a girl by the name of Emily was here. He must have something to do with you."

"Look you sick fuck, I'm telling you to leave the man alone."

"Shut up," spit Ramses. He landed another kick into Evan's side.

"No! This is my land and my shop, Ramses. You're trespassing."

"So what, *ese*? You gonna press charges?" The man laughed bitterly.

"We all have guns trained on each other, but you've got no cover but for your bikes. If someone starts shooting, you'll end up on the bad end of things."

"Says you, *cabron*."

"You give me the *pendejo* and I'll give you back your two men. They're still alive. Your two men for this piece of shit. Then walk away. Nothing good will come of this."

Ramses spit again. "No fuckin' way." He raised his voice, "Do you hear me Aces? I said: NO FUCKING WAY!"

"Listen, Ramses. Before I came here I was with Pez. You know Pez, don't you?"

Ramses face twitched.

"The man speaks for your leadership and the way he was talking, the Hombres too. They already made up their minds about you. They ain't coming to help you. They're just as happy to see us kill each other. Yeah, they want us gone. But they want you gone too."

"You're a fucking liar." The men holding him grunted and pressed against him harder.

Luke winced but refused to show they were hurting him. "I have nothing to gain by lying, Ramses. You'd only find a way to kill me later if I did. I think your best bet is if you leave now, leave Connecticut altogether and get out of the Rojos' face. Maybe if you lie low long enough they'll forget about you."

"That'll never happen, *pendejo*." He grinned wickedly. "We never forgot about you."

"I'm not scared." Luke wasn't and he could see Ramses believed him. "That's one man remembering me, Ramses, keeping that alive. With the way Rojos and Hombres turn over leadership, who knows, in a few years those that care won't be around anymore. Make the smart choice, Ramses."

The one percenter stared at the ground as if thinking things over. He landed another vicious kick into the prostrate Evan. "Let my men go! THEN we'll get out here."

Ramses nodded his head to the two bikers who held Luke. They released him and he bolted for Evan. "Can you move, man?"

"I-I don't know. Something's broke." Evan lay sobbing on the ground like a child. It was almost embarrassing.

Luke draped Evan's arm around his neck and pulled him up.

Evan groaned. "It friggin' hurts," whined Evan.

"Let's move, or it's going to do more than hurt." Luke cast a backward glance to the Rojos leader, who looked on the verge of changing his mind. He pulled Evan the few feet to the clubhouse and up the stairs. The door swung open and Luke let Evan slide down to the floor next to Emily.

"Emily," gasped Evan, still crying.

"What the hell are you doing here, Evan?" Emily shook her head, clearly disgusted. It made Luke smile. He glanced away so the other men wouldn't start laughing.

Evan scrunched his face as if another wave of pain ran through him. "I was looking for you. I thought if you were anywhere, it'd be here with him, and from what the police said, that wasn't safe."

"The police?" said Luke.

"Detective," said Evan, wincing, "Anglotti. He came by my house earlier asking about you. He asked about Emily too, what she was to you."

"Putting two and two together," muttered Luke.

"What?" said Emily.

"Anglotti's been surveilling my shop, but not for the reason he said."

Luke turned and looked over to Aces. "Let the Rojos go, Aces."

"I don't like this," said Aces, crossing his arms over his chest stubbornly.

"Look, you sent me to deal. I made a deal. Let them go."

Aces grunted and finally waved his hand towards the two men propped against the wall. Wolf and Dagger hauled them to their feet and jerked them toward the door. Aces opened it once more, and the Spawn pitched them forward, letting them fall down the stairs. "There! You got your men! Now get the hell out of here!"

"Tell your guys. Tell them we have a deal," yelled Ramses.

Aces leaned toward the open door. "Hold your fire!" he hollered. "They're leaving!"

When the sound of motorcycles rumbling to life, echoed in the hut, everyone inside sighed with relief.

But the crack of a gunfire shot ripped through the clubhouse and Aces, aka Jack Kinney, fell back from the door gasping, holding his chest as blood poured through his fingers.

"Get down!" roared Luke, and he pushed Emily on top of Evan. With a wild swing of his hand he brought one of the clubhouse tables on top of both of them, a vague protection against the bite of flaming bullets.

"Fuck, fuck, fuck," he swore, the sound of his voice nearly drowned in the gunfire exploding from the weapons in the hands of the men at the window, and the roof and the sides of the windows. The Rojos returned fire, shattering the windows of the clubhouse.

In the background, police sirens wailed. The Rojos motorcycles rumbled again, and it sounded as if they were leaving. But they stopped. The gunfire stopped too.

"What's going on?" asked Emily.

"The police," said Luke, "have barricaded the entrance to the gate. The Rojos can't get out."

"Lay down your weapons and come out with your hands up."

"Now they fucking show up," said Pepper exasperated. "George, we're up."

"Right," said George. He stood against the wall, pointing his gun towards Wolf and Dagger. "DEA! Put down your weapons and lay down with your hands on your head."

"Asshole!" snapped Wolf. "You got to help Aces. He's dying there."

Luke moved toward Aces, who gasped.

"Fucker," he wheezed.

"It hit your shoulder, man. You'll be okay."

"I can't breathe." He gasped some more. "My inhaler. Inner pocket."

"Seriously?"

"He's got asthma, man," said Wolf. "He needs his inhaler."

Luke reached for Ace's inside pocket.

"You there!" shouted someone from outside. "Move away from that man! Come out here with your hands up!"

"What's happening, Luke?" asked Pepper.

"A cop's got a rifle on me," said Luke, barely breathing and frozen where he was.

"Do what he says," said Pepper. "Otherwise he's trained to shoot."

Luke stood, holding up his hands while Aces gasped on the floor.

"This man needs medical attention," Luke shouted.

"Out of there! Now!"

Luke gave one last look at Emily. "I love you," he said. Then he stepped out of the doorway.

Emily pushed away the table and moved toward the window, peering out of it. She watched through the clubhouse door as Luke walked down the stairs, arms held over his head. "Be careful, Luke," she whispered.

"On the ground, on the ground!"

Luke sunk to his knees. Ahead of him, Rojos were on the ground.

By the garage he caught a flicker of movement. It happened too fast for Luke to react. A man rose and, in a flash, twisted, pointing a long-range rifle at Luke. The sound of the gunshot echoed off the building, and Luke fell.

"Luke!" screamed Emily as another round of gunfire ripped through the lot.

"Hold your fire!" screamed Pepper through the window "DEA! Hold your fire!"

Finally, the deafening noises stopped. Emily stared in horror at the scene. Men lay in many places on the blacktop, some groaning and moving, others still.

Pepper and George moved out of the building, holding out their badges.

Police rushed the scene, some pointing their weapons, others going to the fallen men, fastening zip ties on the wrists of the men that still moved.

"Luke," cried Emily again, and, heart pounding, she flew out of the building and dropped by him.

"Miss," said a policeman moving to her. "Get away from him."

But Emily ignored the police officer. "No!" she hissed. "He can't die on me now, not after everything we've been through!"

The pain throbbing through his body nearly drove him to pass out. He fought it, trying to be awake to protect Emily. He glanced down in surprise. There was a horrible hole in his gut that was bleeding profusely.

Instinctively, Emily put her hand on the wound, putting pressure on it.

Luke groaned. "Emily?" he said weakly, his eyes fluttering open.

"I absolutely forbid you to die, Luke Wade! We're getting married. Get that through your thick dumb-ass head! We're getting married and you're going to be a father. You can't fuckin' die!"

"Sure, Em," he mumbled. "I'll marry you tomorrow. Just let me sleep now."

"Luke!"

Luke's eyes closed as Emily screamed his name.

EPILOGUE

Emily sucked in a deep breath as Angela handed her the flowers. "Evan's out there," her sister said, her tone and her eyes filled with disapproval.

Emily shrugged. It didn't matter.

"You sure you want to do this?"

Emily smoothed down the fabric of her dress over her expanded stomach. "Do I really have a choice?"

"Well, you could always wait until after the baby comes."

"No. I'll be married when I deliver my child."

"Have it your way, then." Angela smiled. "Still, with everything you've been through, no one would blame you to wait or elope." She winked at her big sister.

Emily took Angela's hand and covered it with her own. "And waste the church date you wrangled from Father Peters for your original wedding plan? Besides, mom and dad are more than happy to give you the biggest May wedding they can afford after this, just to clear the family name." She laughed. "I'll be fine. This is the right thing to do."

"Let's do this then. You've more courage than I'll ever have." Angela hugged Emily, her little body shaking.

Emily didn't blame her. The law enforcement and media attention after the shootout cast a bad light on this whole affair. The New Haven paper even printed a story with the headline, 'Knocked Up Spawn Cutie to Marry'. Her father was never more mortified.

Angela walked before her and opened the door, then led her down the corridor to the inner entrance of the church. Father Peters allowed the ceremony here on the proviso that the wedding itself was small and Emily didn't object. She was too tired these days to handle a big wedding anyway. In the end, it didn't matter.

Emily looked down the long aisle to the man that would be her husband. The organ music struck up and Angela started down the aisle. Emily waited the twenty paces rehearsed and walked after Angela. Despite the fact she knew exactly what she was doing, she had butterflies in her stomach and she found herself on the verge of tears. She kept her head lowered to try to control her hormone-driven emotions. It took longer than she wanted to get here. Father Peters was very insistent that they attend the Pre-Cana classes, the marriage preparation classes required by the church.

Finally, she reached the step that led to the altar and put her foot on it. A hand reached out to hers and steadied her as she stepped up. She looked up to Luke's smiling face. He looked so gorgeous in his tux she couldn't believe that in a few minutes he'd be her husband.

In the long week she waited in the hospital as Luke fought for his life, she said many prayers. One of them was that she'd be standing with Luke at this altar. She'd be forever grateful God had answered them.

Of course, Luke teased her by wearing his new Hades' Spawn jacket to the wedding, the one with the newly added 'vice president' patch over his name. He'd be in charge of the club until Okie got his new trial. The lawyer Luke hired thought he could make a case to get Okie released.

Emily glanced back at the guests, the men of the club who left and recently came back because of the new leadership, and the return to the old one-piece patch. Saks stood next to Luke as best man, looking devilishly handsome. The others, Pepper included, stood in the rows of pews. He hadn't quit the DEA yet, though, because he took the fall for the botched DEA operation, he was consigned to a desk job. But he still worked with Luke in the shop on the weekends.

Emily smiled. All the members behaved and kept their colors out of the church, despite their teasing. But she suspected they'd appear at the informal reception at the patched-up clubhouse.

Evan sat in a back pew looking miserable. Time had healed the injuries to his body. She wasn't so sure about his heart. But weddings are public occasions, you can't stop people from showing up at the church.

Mrs. Diggerty gave her the brightest smile imaginable, pleased as she could be to be invited to this intimate gathering. Emily could do no less. She owed her so much.

She glanced at her mother and her father sitting in the front pew. Her mother gave her a weak smile while her father sat stoned faced. She knew Sam Dougherty appeared under protest, but in the face of the priest's blessing, there was little he could do. That didn't matter anyway. There was nothing now to keep Emily from marrying the man she loved.

"Shall we being?" Father Peters asked.

"Hey," Luke whispered and Emily turned back to him. He wiped away her tear with his hand. "What's this?"

"I'm just so damned happy."

Father Peters cleared his throat and gave her a disapproving look.

"Sorry, Father," she whispered, her cheeks burning.

He nodded, pressing his lips tight to keep the smile twitching at the corners of his mouth from curling upwards. Father Peters cleared his throat once more. "Let us begin again, shall we?"

And they did.

THE END

...

unless you want to find out if Luke's past catches up with him, or who Emily's father is...

NOW AVAILABLE!

NEW
One Christmas Night
Hades' Spawn Christmas Novella
Now Available!

Luke and Emily have each other, and their toddler son, but every other relationship in their lives is strained—the result of the violent events revolving around the Spawn and the club's president two years before.

When the president of Hades' Spawn, Oakie Walker, insists Luke and Emily host the club's Christmas Party, Luke's not very happy. Though he was reinstated as a member of the Spawn, and maintains their clubhouse, he spends only the time he has to with the club.

Emily's adoptive father, Sam Dougherty, makes no bones that biker Luke is not good enough for his daughter, while her biological father, Rob, wants to get closer to her and his grandson and no one but Emily is happy about it. Add to the mix that the president of a rival motorcycle club, the Rojos, does everything he can to create the impression that Luke will join his gang, and you have a recipe for one explosive Christmas party.

Can Luke and Emily negotiate the tricky currents of the demands from those around them? Or will it damage their relationship if they do?

NEW SERIES Coming January 2017!

EXCERPT INCLUDED!

Making Her His

Saks' Story

Anthony Parks, AKA Saks straddles two worlds and neither one is very reputable. One is as a motorcycle mechanic and Road Captain of the Hades Spawn, a none too squeaky clean motorcycle club. The other is as the scion of an organized crime family who wants him to join the family business, something he is loathed to do.

Recent events with the Spawn has soured his community reputation, and while certain women like bad boys, those kind of women are not who Saks is looking for. Add pressure from his family that "it is time to marry" Saks is faced with an impossible situation.

His wise-guy uncle proposes an arranged marriage between Saks and the daughter of a dom from another crime family. And when he meets a mysterious blonde that shows him love at first sight is possible, he knows that he could never accept his uncle proposal. Now he would just have to figure out a way to tell Uncle Vits without getting excommunicated from the family or putting the Spawn in the crosshairs of a powerful crime organization. While he is doing that he has to find the woman who has stolen his heart.

Christina

Christina Marie Serafini decided a long time ago that her loving but paternalistic family wasn't going to determine the course of her life. She had no desire to get mixed up in any of the many legal and illegal businesses her family owned. Chrissy had earned a Masters in Business and Communications on her own dime, and she just landed her dream job of Director of Marketing for an up and coming business.

Marriage and a family isn't in her game plan right now and when she did marry it was going to be a respectable man. When her grandfather announced he had arranged a marriage for her with "a nice Italian man," Christina goes ballistic. She wasn't going to marry anyone, let alone someone chosen for her. She certainly wouldn't marry a member from another crime family. Chrissy could only imagine what kind of opportunistic carogna would agree to marry a woman he never met.

Urged by her sister to at least check him out, she goes to his family's bar to confirm her suspicions. That's when she finds a handsome biker that knows exactly how to send her emotions and body into overdrive. But realizing the hunky man is the one her grandfather wants to marry sends her into flight mode even though he haunts her dreams.

Once he finds her can Saks convince the woman of his dreams to look past his family connections to take a chance on a lowly motorcycle mechanic? And if he does, can he look past hers?

COMING January 2017

Bestselling Author
LEXY TIMMS
MAKING HER His
BEATING THE BIKER #1

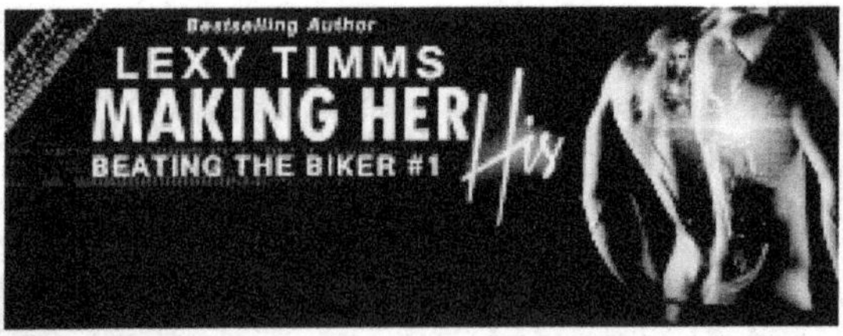

Making Her His - CHAPTER 1

Saks' Sunday Dinner

"Don't you have a place to be?" His cousin, John Rocco, bartender of the Red Bull, slid a beer toward Saks with his eyebrows arched.

Saks sat at the bar of the Red Bull, which was a second home to him. Even the new clubhouse of the Hades Spawn didn't hold the memories of the Red Bull. He flicked his eyes up to the rafters of the bar where brightly colored bras hung, evidence of the watering hole's rambunctious reputation.

"Yeah. Sunday dinner."

"So?" said John.

Saks shrugged. "So?"

"Aren't you going to be late?"

"In case you haven't noticed, dinner is served twenty-four-seven at my mom's house."

John gave him a "you're-not-getting-the-point" glance and turned to another customer.

Of course, Saks got the point. It was about respect. Uncle Vits, the head of the Rocco family, was going to be there. One did not disrespect the man by showing up late.

But there was something about this day that put Sakes on guard. Part of it was the way his mother insisted that he show up rather than "hang around with that gang of yours." Another was how John made a big deal about Saks being here instead of his parent's house. He didn't know what was going on.

It's not that he didn't love his family. But the fact was he was more than wary of the organized crime aspect of it. He wasn't drawn to their activities, like so many of his other cousins, and he didn't want to make his life around it either. He'd seen too many of his uncles or cousins incarcerated for family crimes taking their jail time as a badge of honor. He didn't think it was either smart or honorable to be involved in illegal activities. His mother backed him on this against his uncle, or rather granduncle, and made sure that Saks' father didn't drag him into the family business.

As a result, Saks lived as an outsider in his own family. Conversations stopped when he entered the room. He didn't hang out with his cousins.

Which was why the Hades Spawn was so important to him.

Well, that, and riding bikes.

Those two things, plus working for Luke Wade, owner of Central Valley Bike Repair, as a motorcycle mechanic made up his life. Unfortunately, his life didn't include a steady girlfriend, which was why he was sitting here at noon on Sunday in a motorcycle hangout bar, killing time.

"Hello."

A pretty brunette slid onto the stool next to him. Her too tight tee that was cut at the midriff advertised what she was looking for.

"I haven't seen you here before," said the brunette with a flash of extra-white teeth.

Saks almost chuckled. "Then you haven't been here often enough," he said

"Buy a girl a drink?" she said.

She didn't even wait to be offered one. Saks didn't like brazen women like this and he could guess what was going to happen next. And it did. She slid her hand on thigh inching her way to his inner leg.

"Which bike out there is yours?" she purred. "I'd love to have a ride."

Of course she would. And she wasn't thinking about riding his bike either.

"John, give the lady here what she wants-on me," said Saks. He then twisted away on the stool.

"You're leaving?" she said in bewilderment.

"I have a family thing. Sorry. Another time." Like no time ever. When he was younger and more impulsive, he would have taken the woman to bed in a heartbeat. But now he was growing older bedding anonymous women lost its shine. At Luke and Emily's wedding that he got an inkling he wanted what they had. Seeing the looks of utter love they gave each other, and watching over these past two years how they stood together against every challenge, he came to realize what he wanted that. Lover. Partner. Best friend.

That would not be this woman, who could be had for the price of a beer and a motorcycle ride.

"See you around," said the woman.

"Sure," said Saks.

Walking away from that woman ease the queasiness in his stomach she elicited. The rumble of his bike's engine shook away the sleazy feeling that clung to him from the woman's touch. Pushing out on the highway eased his mind. His engine sang a song to him, a serenade created from the precision action of pistons perfectly timed to send its life's blood through the engine. Though he drove on blacktop, he felt connected to the earth, wheels on road, sliding seamlessly toward his destination. If it weren't for his roiling thoughts about the family dinner, he would be perfectly at peace.

"Anthony!" said his mother as Saks entered the kitchen door. "Finally you are here. Your Uncle Vits was going crazy thinking you weren't going to show."

Saks kissed his mother on the cheek and took in the familiar Italian restaurant smells of his mother's kitchen. Sauce was bubbling on the stove, and fresh baked Italian bread sat sliced on the table. He reached for a slice but his mother slapped his hand away.

"Of course, I'm here for Sunday dinner. I always am, aren't I? And why is he so anxious today?"

"Here," his mother said as she handed him a platter of fried calamari, "take this to the table."

"Don't you need some help?" he said studying her face. Her bright brown eyes were more lined than usual, and her face seemed drained of color. "You're looking tired, Ma. You should sit down."

"Sush!" she said waving him away. "Terri is helping me."

"Where is my sister?"

"Here I am, Anthony," said Terri. She stood at the top of the basement stair with a long flat tray in her hands. On the tray were freshly made ravioli ready to be cooked.

Saks set down the calamari on the kitchen table.

"Let me help you," he said.

Terri rolled her eyes. "I'm perfectly capable of carrying a tray, thank you very much."

"Sorry," said Saks sarcastically, "for trying to be a gentleman."

Terri stuck her tongue at him while she walked past.

"Take off that jacket," his mother said. Her voice was full of disapproval as she eyed his Hades Spawn leather. "Your uncle will have a fit if he sees it."

Saks shrugged off the cut and hung it carefully on a kitchen chair. "He's good with the club, Mom," he said.

"No," she said. "He tolerates it for your sake." She stared at distaste the club's patch, a skull over a pair of wings. His mothered fingered the leather pulling the front of the jacket closer for her to see. "And what is this? Saks?"

"I've told you before. That's my club name."

"And why do they call you Saks?"

"Because, mom," said Terri setting the ravioli tray on the counter, "Look at him. Khakis? White button down? He dresses better than the rest of them, like Saks of Fifth Avenue? Get it."

His mother rolled her dark eyes again.

"Named after a store. What is wrong with those people?"

"Those people," said Saks, "are my friends." He scooped up a piece of fried calamari and scarfed it down.

"Hey," protested Terri. Saks grinned at her.

"That's for the table," said his mother. "And take it now before it gets cold."

"You need to sit."

"I'll sit after I cook the ravioli."

"I'll do it, ma," said Terri. "Go sit down with dinner. The water boiling is now. It will take five minutes."

Marie Parks grumbled, but she picked up the basket of bread. Saks walked behind her into the dining room where the curtains were drawn tight giving the room a gloomy air. Any other day they would be pulled apart letting the sun in, but today Uncle Vits was visiting.

Uncle Vits sat at the head of the table facing the kitchen while Saks' father stood pouring a glass of wine. The elderly man sat hunched in the chair. He was shorter than most men, a had a rounded belly that led him to play Santa at Christmas for the family. But his sharp, predatory blue eyes commanded the room, giving the distinct impression that anyone that crossed him would feel his wrath.

Vito Rocco was in fact his granduncle, not his uncle which is why Saks' last name was the very Anglo-Saxon name of Parks. Saks' father, Carmello "Whit" Parks, half-Italian from his mother's side, married into the Rocco family by taking Maria Rocco as his wife. His actual grandfather, long since passed was what they euphemistically called "an associate" of Uncle Vits who was "capo" or boss of a good slice of Connecticut. Much of the rest was under the control of their bitter rivals, the Serafini.

"Anthony," said Uncle Vits, "good to see you. Sit. Sit."

Sakes resisted the urge to roll his eyes. It was normal for Vits to act like he was the king in everyone else's house. Saks never understood why other people put up with it, but no one questioned Vito Rocco.

But another thing that was strange about this gathering was that only Vits, not any other member of the extended family sat at the long table. This was more than unusual. It was suspicious. What was going on?

Saks' father poured him a glass of wine as his mother took her place at the head of the table. Terri walked in with the bowl of ravioli. With a spoon she ladled over generous portions to Uncle Vits, her father, her mother and then Saks.

"Hand me that gravy, there, Anthony," said Vits. "And the bread too."

Like many old Italians Vits called tomato sauce gravy. Saks reached over the large salad, the bowl of meatballs, and another of sausage and peppers to grab both items and passed them to his granduncle.

"Grace," reminded his mother. "Anthony, please."

Saks never knew why his mother always chose him to say grace except for maybe she had hoped he would become a priest. Her hope died, however, when Saks refused to go to the seminary college she wanted him to attend. But to get dinner going he made the sign of the cross and the others followed.

"Bless us, oh Lord, and these thy gifts which come from your bounty, through Christ, our Lord. Amen."

"Amen," all at the table affirmed.

Vits laced the ravioli with sauce and took a bite.

"Perfect, Maria, perfect as always. Just like my sainted mother's."

Saks' mother smiled at the compliment.

"Thank you, Uncle Vits."

"And Anthony," said Vits, "how are things for you, eh?"

"Everything's fine," said Saks noncommittally.

"You getting out and having fun?"

"I hang out with my club."

"Yes," hissed Vits. "Your *familia* not good enough for you, eh? But you spend time with that motorcycle club, where Icherra's nephew—"

Vits was referring to Luke, whose uncle, Raymondo Icherra was a Mexican drug lord. But Luke, like Saks, eschewed his criminal family.

"Now, Uncle Vits," chided Terri gently. "This is a nice family gathering, right? Anthony likes his friends."

Vits always had a soft spot for Terri, who he often said was the spitting image of his mother. For this reason she could say things to him that others couldn't.

"Yes, yes," he said waving his hands as if to breeze away his rancorous comments. "A nice family gathering. Sorry." Without a breath he continued the conversation, "So, have you thought about marriage, Anthony?"

"Of course I've thought about it. But I haven't found the right girl."

"So you aren't dating anyone serious?"

"No," said Saks slowly wondering where this intrusive conversation was leading.

"Well, good. There's nice young woman I'd like you to meet. Very pretty. And smart. Very smart. You like that I know."

"Thanks, Uncle Vits, but I can get my own dates."

"No. You don't understand, Anthony. I think she'd make a good wife for you."

Vits spoke with the authority of a Capo, a boss, and Saks looked around at his family's faces. Terri smirked, her mother smiled and his father looked off innocently to the side. But his father, his mother and his sister were no innocents. They were all part of this conspiracy.

"Wife?" said Saks, his voice rising. "Wife? What have you done, Uncle Vits?"

The capo stared at his fingernails.

"Nothing. Not much. Just made a little proposal to the Serafini."

"What!" said Saks jumping to his feet as cold fear rushed through him. "The Serafini? Our rivals?"

"Sit down, Anthony," said Vits dismissively. "It will be good. Good for you. Good for her. Good for business."

Saks sank to his chair under the weight of this mother and father's disapproving glares and knew there was only one thing that was good about this. He was good and fucked.

~ End of Excerpt ~

More by Lexy Timms:

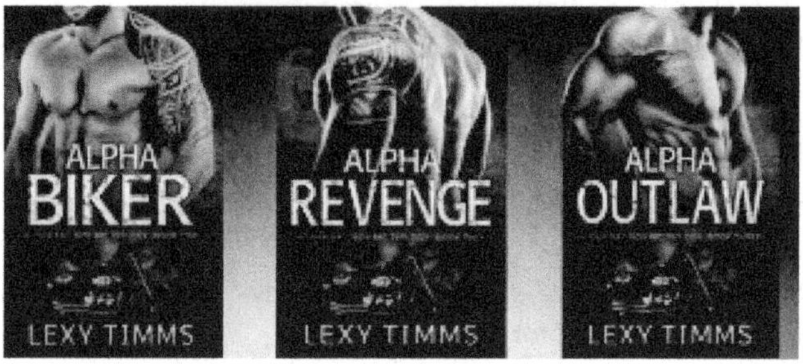

Alpha Biker

Loyalties will be tested and lives will be lost.

Jace is a brother, now turned president, of the Cerberus Legends Motorcycle club. It wasn't by choice. The presidency came at the cost of his best friend's, Fork's, life. Fork was shot by a rival motorcycle gang, the Chiron Knights. Jace is forced to finish the job. It tears holes inside of him bigger than any bullet could do.

He finds comfort in the arms (and legs) of Classic, a bar dancer at the Iron Hog. Classic belongs to one of the Chiron Knight brothers and Jace must immediately choose bros before hoes.

When Classic is critically injured while riding her motorbike, it's clear the Chiron Knights tried to take her out of the picture. Disgusted by their ruthless antics, Jace declares war against the Knights.

Loyalties are tested and lives will be lost, all in the name of the brotherhood of the road.

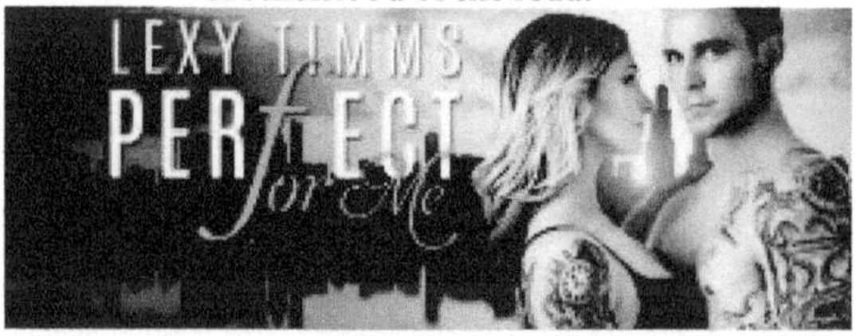

Perfect For Me

They say love comes in all forms.

The city of Pittsburgh keeps its streets safe, partly thanks to Lt. Grady Rivers. The police officer is fiercely intelligent who specializes in undercover operations. It is this set of skills that are sought by New York's finest. Grady is thrown from his hometown onto the New York City underworld in order to stop one of the largest drug rings in the northeast. The NYPD task him with uncovering the identity of the organization's mysterious leader, Dean. It will take all of his cunning to stop this deadly drug lord.

Danger lurks around every corner and comes in many shapes. While undercover, he meets a beauty named Lara. An equally intelligent woman and twice as fearless, she works for a local drug dealer who has ties to the organization. Their sorted pasts have these two become close, and soon they develop feelings for one another. But this is not a "Romeo and Juliet" love story, as the star-crossed lovers fight to survive the deadly streets. Grady treads the thin line between the love he feels for her, and his duties as an officer. Will he get in too deep?

Perfect for Me is book 1 of the Undercover Series. It will end on a cliff hanger

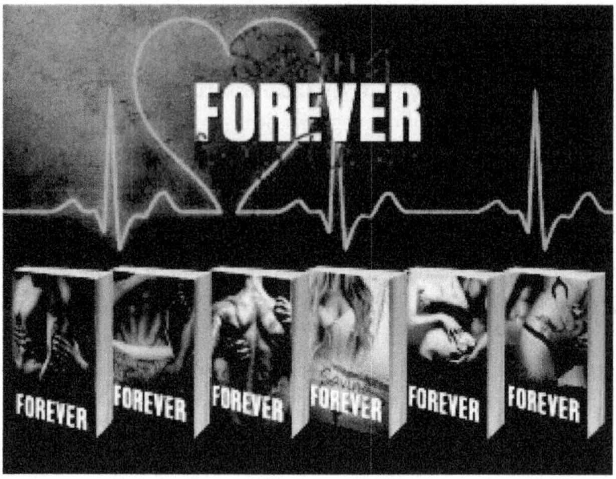

Book One is FREE!

Sometimes the heart needs a different kind of saving... find out if Charity Thompson will find a way of saving forever in this hospital setting Best-Selling Romance by Lexy Timms

Charity Thompson wants to save the world, one hospital at a time. Instead of finishing med school to become a doctor, she chooses a different path and raises money for hospitals – new wings, equipment, whatever they need. Except there is one hospital she would be happy to never set foot in again—her fathers. So of course he hires her to create a gala for his sixty-fifth birthday. Charity can't say no. Now she is working in the one place she doesn't want to be. Except she's attracted to Dr. Elijah Bennet, the handsome playboy chief.

Will she ever prove to her father that's she's more than a med school dropout? Or will her attraction to Elijah keep her from repairing the one thing she desperately wants to fix?

** This is NOT Erotica. It's Romance and a love story. **

* This is Part 1 of a Five book Romance Series. It does end on a cliffhanger*

Heart of the Battle
LEXY TIMMS

Heart of the Battle Series

Celtic Viking

Book 1 is FREE

In a world plagued with darkness, she would be his salvation.

No one gave Erik a choice as to whether he would fight or not. Duty to the crown belonged to him, his father's legacy remaining beyond the grave.

Taken by the beauty of the countryside surrounding her, Linzi would do anything to protect her father's land. Britain is under attack and Scotland is next. At a time she should be focused on suitors, the men of her country have gone to war and she's left to stand alone.

Love will become available, but will passion at the touch of the enemy unravel her strong hold first?

Fall in love with this Historical Celtic Viking Romance.

* There are 3 books in this series. Book 1 will end on a cliff hanger.

*Note: this is NOT erotica. It is a romance and a love story.

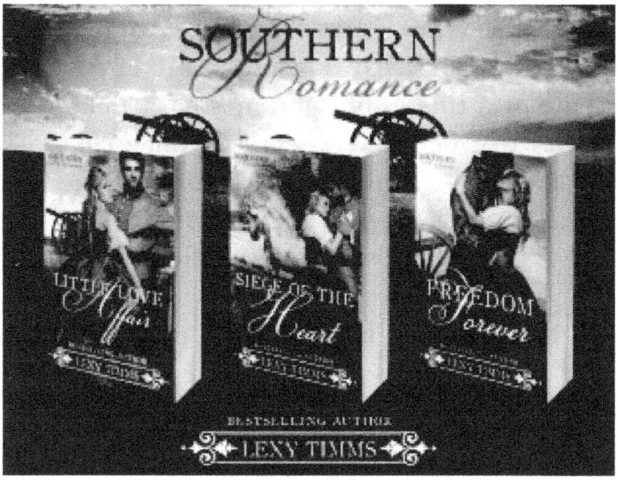

Knox Township, August 1863.

Little Love Affair, Book 1 in the Southern Romance series, by bestselling author Lexy Timms

Sentiments are running high following the battle of Gettysburg, and although the draft has not yet come to Knox, "Bloody Knox" will claim lives the next year as citizens attempt to avoid the Union draft. Clara's brother Solomon is missing, and Clara has been left to manage the family's farm, caring for her mother and her younger sister, Cecelia.

Meanwhile, wounded at the battle of Monterey Pass but still able to escape Union forces, Jasper and his friend Horace are lost and starving. Jasper wants to find his way back to the Confederacy, but feels honor-bound to bring Horace back to his family, though the man seems reluctant.

NOTE: This is romance series, book 1 of 4

The Recruiting Trip

Aspiring college athlete Aileen Nessa is finding the recruiting process beyond daunting. Being ranked #10 in the world for the 100m hurdles at the age of eighteen is not a fluke, even though she believes that one race, where everything clinked magically together, might be. American universities don't seem to think so. Letters are pouring in from all over the country.

As she faces the challenge of differentiating between a college's genuine commitment to her or just empty promises from talent-seeking coaches, Aileen heads to the University of Gatica, a Division One school, on a recruiting trip. Her best friend dares who to go just to see the cute guys on the school's brochure.

The university's athletic program boasts one of the top hurdlers in the country. Tyler Jensen is the school's NCAA champion in the hurdles and Jim Thorpe recipient for top defensive back in football. His incredible blue-green eyes, confident smile and rock hard six pack abs mess with Aileen's concentration.

His offer to take her under his wing, should she choose to come to Gatica, is a temping proposition that has her wondering if she might be with an angel or making a deal with the devil himself.

COMING SOON:

justice series
JUSTICE
JUSTICE
LEXY TIMMS

Fire HOUSE
ROMANCE
CAUGHT
FLAMES
BURNING
DESIRE
BESTSELLING AUTHOR
LEXY TIMMS

ONE YOU CAN'T
Forget
BESTSELLING AUTHOR
LEXY TIMMS
ONE THAT GOT
Away
BESTSELLING AUTHOR
LEXY TIMMS
ONE THAT CAME
Back
BESTSELLING AUTHOR
LEXY TIMMS
ONE YOU NEVER
Leave
BESTSELLING AUTHOR
LEXY TIMMS

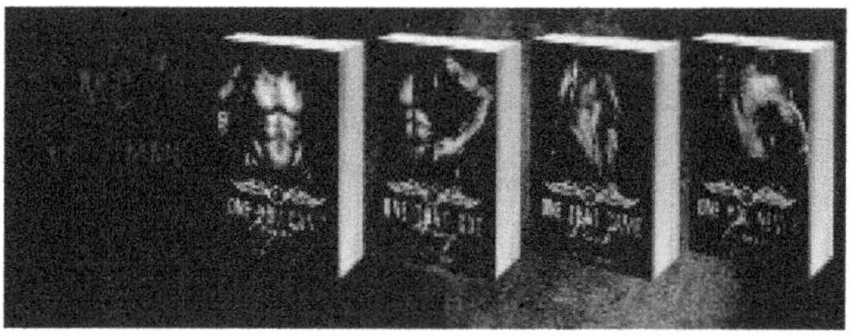

Hades' Spawn Motorcycle Club Series

One You Can't Forget

Book 1

One That Got Away

Book 2

One That Came Back

Book 3

One You Never Leave

Book 4

Find Lexy Timms:

Lexy Timms Newsletter:
http://eepurl.com/9i0vD
Lexy Timms Facebook Page:
https://www.facebook.com/SavingForever
Lexy Timms Website:
http://lexytimms.wix.com/savingforever

HADES' SPAWN
MC
ONE YOU CAN'T
Forget
BESTSELLING AUTHOR
LEXY TIMMS

HADES' SPAWN
MC
#1
ONE THAT GOT
Away
BESTSELLING AUTHOR
LEXY TIMMS

HADES' SPAWN
MC
#3
ONE THAT CAME
Back
BESTSELLING AUTHOR
LEXY TIMMS

HADES' SPAWN
MC
ONE YOU NEVER
Leave
BESTSELLING AUTHOR
LEXY TIMMS

Don't miss out!

Click the button below and you can sign up to receive emails whenever Lexy Timms publishes a new book. There's no charge and no obligation.

Sign Me Up!

https://books2read.com/r/B-A-NNL-UHCH

Connecting independent readers to independent writers.

Did you love *One That Came Back*? Then you should read *Saving Forever - Part 1* by Lexy Timms!

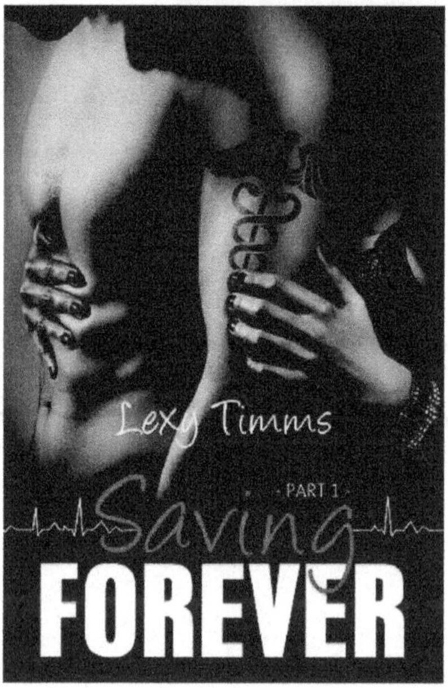

From Best Selling Author, Lexy Timms comes a hospital romance, you won't be able to put down.

Charity Thompson wants to save the world, one hospital at a time. Instead of finishing med school to become a doctor, she chooses a different path and raises money for hospitals - new wings, equipment, whatever they need. Except there is one hospital she would be happy to never set foot in again--her fathers. So of course he hires her to plan a gala event for his sixty-fifth birthday. Charity can't say no. Now she is working in the one place she doesn't want to be.

Except she's attracted to Dr. Elijah Bennet, the handsome playboy chief. Will she ever prove to her father that she's more than a med school dropout? Or will her attraction to Elijah keep her from repairing the one thing she desperately wants to fix?

**this is NOT Erotica. It's a love story and romance that'll have you routing all the way for Charity

***This is an EIGHT book series, all your questions won't be answered in part 1*

Also by Lexy Timms

Alpha Bad Boy Motorcycle Club Triology
Alpha Biker

Conquering Warrior Series
Ruthless

Diamond in the Rough Anthology
Billionaire Rock
Billionaire Rock - part 2

Dominating PA Series
Her Personal Assistant - Part 1
Her Personal Assistant - Part 2
Her Personal Assistant - Part 3
Her Personal Assistant Box Set

Firehouse Romance Series
Caught in Flames
Burning With Desire
Craving the Heat
Firehouse Romance Complete Collection

Fortune Riders MC Series
Billionaire Biker
Billionaire Ransom
Billionaire Misery

Hades' Spawn Motorcycle Club
One You Can't Forget
One That Got Away

One That Came Back
One You Never Leave
Hades' Spawn MC Complete Series

Heart of the Battle Series
Celtic Viking
Celtic Rune
Celtic Mann
Heart of the Battle Series Box Set

Justice Series
Seeking Justice
Finding Justice
Chasing Justice
Pursuing Justice
Justice - Complete Series

Love You Series
Love Life: Billionaire Dance School Hot Romance
Need Love
My Love

Managing the Bosses Series
The Boss
The Boss Too
Who's the Boss Now
Love the Boss
I Do the Boss
Wife to the Boss
Employed by the Boss
Brother to the Boss
Senior Advisor to the Boss
Forever the Boss
Gift for the Boss - Novella 3.5

Christmas With the Boss

Moment in Time

Highlander's Bride

Victorian Bride

Modern Day Bride

A Royal Bride

Forever the Bride

R&S Rich and Single Series

Alex Reid

Parker

Saving Forever

Saving Forever - Part 1

Saving Forever - Part 2

Saving Forever - Part 3

Saving Forever - Part 4

Saving Forever - Part 5

Saving Forever - Part 6

Saving Forever Part 7

Saving Forever - Part 8

Southern Romance Series

Little Love Affair

Siege of the Heart

Freedom Forever

Soldier's Fortune

Tattooist Series

Confession of a Tattooist

Surrender of a Tattooist

Heart of a Tattooist

Tennessee Romance

Whisky Lullaby
Whisky Melody
Whisky Harmony

The Debt
The Debt: Part 1 - Damn Horse
The Debt: Complete Collection

The University of Gatica Series
The Recruiting Trip
Faster
Higher
Stronger
Dominate
No Rush

T.N.T. Series
Troubled Nate Thomas - Part 1
Troubled Nate Thomas - Part 2
Troubled Nate Thomas

Undercover Series
Perfect For Me
Perfect For You
Perfect For Us

Unknown Identity Series
Unknown
Unexposed
Unpublished

Standalone
Wash
Loving Charity
Summer Lovin'

Christmas Magic: A Romance Anthology
Love & College
Billionaire Heart
First Love
Frisky and Fun Romance Box Collection
Managing the Bosses Box Set #1-3